Maid IN CHELSEA

Cleaning for the rich sure beats a relationship that sucks.

Andrene Low

That Seventies Series – Comprising Heels and a Tiara, Friday Night Fever, Brush With Fame, Strapped for Cash, Out of Bounds, Maid in Chelsea and Filthy Rich.

ISBN: 978-0-9951389-4-0

1

This isn't how Vivienne planned her life. Some parts are bang on, while others are unmitigated disasters. Take Kenny. At the outset, he'd looked so good and was her experiment of going 'down market'.

How soon his rock hard abs had softened, along with the rest of him. The only thing hard about him these days is his attitude towards her.

She isn't so much beaten; as browbeaten. Worn down over the preceding seven years and never able to meet Kenny's exacting standards. The longer he's unemployed, the higher these standards become, until she isn't sure there's anything she can do to be deemed successful in his eyes. His meals are too hot, too cold, late. The house is untidy, too tidy and full of tat.

The litany of perceived sins is endless.

One bright spot in her life is her students, not that she ever talks to Kenny about them. If he had any idea how much she loves being a teacher, he'd find some way of spoiling it for her.

No, she'll happily fake lousy days at work and feral kids to keep him in the dark. He'll never know that her hours in the classroom are all that's helping her keep it together.

Looking out at her students, she waits until she has their attention, well as much as is possible at three o'clock on a Friday. "Right, class. Don't forget our field trip to the Museum of London on Monday. If you haven't already given me one, make sure you bring a note from mum or dad to say it's okay. Oh, and don't forget your lunch and some money for the tube."

The other teachers looked at her like she was bonkers when she'd first talked about taking her pint-sized league of nations on an outing into the city. "It'll be like herding cats," was the most popular refrain, followed closely by "You'll lose half of them, mark my words." It was the second sentiment, uttered with such glee that told Vivienne how much her fellow teachers loathed kids.

Sure, her lot can be a challenge at times, ranging as they do from recent arrivals from warmer climes, right through to the 'wide boys' in training from East London. She doesn't need to worry about those ruffians unless it's them nicking stuff from the museum gift shop.

And if they become separated from the group, they'll no doubt make it home in better time than Vivienne and the rest of the class. That they'd more than likely 'borrow' a car for the trip is her biggest concern.

At seven and eight years, they're too short to reach the accelerator, let alone the brakes. However, Viv isn't naïve enough to think this won't stop them from giving it a whirl.

As expected, the class empties like a burst hot-water bottle seconds after the bell, until only a couple of nervous souls are left behind, anguish writ large on their faces. "What are you worried about, Alfred?" Such a big and regal name for so small an Indian boy, the choice of moniker testament to how strong the English influence still is on the Indian sub-continent. As always, whenever she speaks to him, he is sufficiently tongue-tied that a coherent response is ruled out.

Vivienne takes over their conversation in such a way that all he needs do is nod or shake. "Did you get your permission slip?" This is solemnly handed over. "And what about money for the tube?" He unzips his pencil case and shows her a handful of coins and even a few notes stuffed in the bottom with all the pencil shavings. There's more than enough to get him both to and from the museum, even if he wants to catch a cab. "What about lunch?"

This is when Vivienne knows she's found the

sticking point. While all the other kids turn up to school with an assortment of sandwiches and junk food, Albert's mum proves herself to be a culinary whiz. The poor kid is saddled each day with a stack of stainless containers that lock together with a band that forms a handle.

There are never less than three courses and consuming those takes up most of his lunch break. This is in comparison to his classmates gaily stuffing sandwiches in their gobs in between running around and screaming.

"You know, you've got enough money there that you could buy a sandwich if you wanted. It could be our secret." Okay, so Vivienne isn't as altruistic as she's making out. Better to get the boy onto the tube without a high-rise of oily Indian cuisine than have to deal with it out in the real world.

She answers questions from the other Nervous Nelly before getting on with tidying her classroom in readiness to head home for the weekend. She's wiping the blackboard clean with a damp cloth when Gareth Jones, upper school maths and science, pops his head through the door. "What on earth did you say to Albert Chaudhary? The boy just skipped down the hallway."

"Hah, told him we'd leave the Tandoori Tower of Doom behind on the field trip and buy a sandwich for lunch instead."

"Excellent, bags first dibs on his lunch." Gareth doesn't bother waiting for a response, taking it as a given and leaving Vivienne to finish up.

Spinning out the tidy-up, Viv is still careful not to tarry too long. If she's late home with Kenny's Friday-night Chinese, her weekend will be hell from beginning to end, rather than hell in places.

One plus is that the Chinese restaurant is near the station at the other end of her journey. She used to have a car, but Kenny said she needed to sell it to help fund their lifestyle after he hurt his back badly enough he couldn't work.

It didn't take her long to see that maintaining their lifestyle involved him buying the biggest telly he could find, and one where the screen had miraculously remained intact when it fell off the back of the lorry.

Even more miraculous was how he'd managed to carry this monster into the house without help. There'd been no point asking where the rest of the funds went, with his dire case of brewer's droop clearly identifying the recipient as the pub on the corner.

Viv's relieved to step straight onto a tube for home rather than waiting, something that could have made her late. Likewise, there's no slowing in her journey when she swings by the Flying

Dragon, her usual order already stacked and waiting on the counter. Also as per routine, she hands over a ten pound note and gets exact change in return.

Rather than put the coins back in her purse she slides them into the pocket of coat, only to be retrieved so she can drop them through the letter slot in her neighbour's door.

“I'm home.” Viv doesn't need to announce this, but it doesn't stop her. Better to let Kenny know her whereabouts. He doesn't like surprises, something she's learned the hard way.

The only response is a sleepy grunt from the general direction of the sitting room; Viv imagines the arse-shaped dent in the couch already. She'll be lucky if he manages to drag himself upright for dinner, preferring to lie in splendour and eat with his hands ‘like the natives’.

Unfortunately, any resemblance to the natives ends there. Viv knows from watching her students eat that they don't end up with food smeared all over them. And especially not on a filthy singlet that's deemed acceptable attire for dining at home. Only by studiously keeping her eyes glued to the telly is Viv able to eat her meal with any semblance of appetite.

The plastic bag of takeaway containers balanced precariously on the hall table, Viv ditches her trench coat and handbag, slinging them over the newel post on the stairs to save time.

As per routine she nips through to the kitchen, levers all the tops free and slaps them down higgledy-piggledy on a tray. Kenny is all about self-serve, even if half the time he doesn't bother with the plate she gives him, preferring to eat straight from the containers. Doesn't he know how hard it is to get sweet and sour sauce out of Axminster carpet?

"It's about effing time. I'm starved." Kenny stabs his finger at the small coffee table next to the couch, indicating Viv should put his tray there and be bloody quick about it.

As tempting as it is to smash the tray over his head, she puts it down on the china cabinet and sets about clearing the coffee table of empty beer bottles.

Having tidied up after dinner, Viv feigns a headache caused by "those snot-nosed kids she's unlucky enough to be saddled with" and heads for bed. She's not tired, but going to bed and losing herself in a book is bliss. Better this than being stuck in the sitting room with Kenny farting loudly in response to the spicy food he's hoovered his way through.

Viv knows from experience that by ten o'clock, the atmosphere in the front room will be toxic, although never enough to asphyxiate him, unfortunately.

Tonight is different. She's not even a couple of pages into her book when she hears Kenny on the stairs. Her stomach knots in response.

Surely he won't try for sex tonight.

All it does is make him angry.

Kenny grabs Viv around the throat, yanking her face inches from his. "You useless slag. You being built like a bloke, that's what screws up big Kenny." He shoves her away as though she's a piece of dirt, further reinforcing this with more spit-laden invective.

If this wasn't enough, he jams his foot in the middle of her back and shunts her out of bed. Actual physical violence is a step-up even for Kenny and she tumbles off the mattress, landing hard on her hands and knees.

"You effing bitch, if ya can't get me hard, ya can sleep on the sodding couch."

Yet again Kenny having as much substance as a piece of fried fish left in the steamer for too long is all her fault. He used to like her height and smaller breasts; now he's using them as an excuse for his lack of performance. Faced with yet another night on a couch still infused with the smell of second-hand chow mein, Viv snaps.

She hoped to have more time to prepare, but

if she waits any longer, she risks being hurt far worse than tonight's bumps and bruises. Her biggest disappointment will be letting her students down on Monday.

But, if she's getting out, it's now or never and the break needs to be a clean one. All going well Kenny will be comatose before eight o'clock tonight and so this is as good a time as any to escape.

There's no way she can get dressed with him watching her through slit eyes. The jig would be up then. Instead she grabs her dressing gown off the end of the bed and scurries out of the room as though to do his bidding.

She has no intention of spending another night on their lumpy, stinky couch. Instead she makes her way downstairs and out to the small laundry in the converted coal shed. A quick rummage through the dirty washing has her in possession of a skirt and blouse that will pass muster, just, likewise a bra and knickers.

Back in the hallway she wastes no time dressing, before grabbing her coat off the newel post and shrugging into it. She then buttons it up tight and belts it even tighter. Thank goodness she didn't think to take her coat and handbag upstairs as she usually would.

Viv still has her hand on the highly polished

brass knocker on her neighbour's front door when it swings soundlessly open. "I've been expecting you, love. It's time."

That Cecily, her elderly neighbour, has been privy to her and Kenny's 'lovemaking' comes as no surprise. The walls are paper-thin, allowing cold drafts and whispered conversations to find their way through with equal ease. They don't stand a chance when faced with Kenny's spleen-ridden coupling.

Viv waits on the footpath that's right next to the front door rather than follow her neighbour into the narrow hallway. There she sways gently and hugs herself tight in a futile attempt to stop her trembling. This isn't down to the chill of the evening, but rather a fear of the unknown.

Cecily is soon back and handing over the small suitcase Viv has left there. She's taken months filling it with charity shop finds rather than risk packing her own clothes. Anything to lessen the chance of Kenny noticing her usually meagre wardrobe is even thinner on the rail.

"Are you sure you won't stay here tonight, love?" says her neighbour, grabbing a bulging fabric pouch off the bottom step. She hands this over to Viv, with the coins inside rattling reassuringly.

Viv hefts this into her purse, causing the shoulder straps to drag in protest. "I think it's best I get as far away as possible." She's going to have to be a lot further away from Kenny than next door when he wakes in the morning. "Have you got the letters?"

"Oh. Oh, yes, I have." Cecily collects a bundle of letters from the drawer of a small table that sits snugly against one wall of the hallway.

Viv slides these into her oversized shoulder bag and gives Cecily a tight hug. "I'll be in touch."

Looking up at the smart hotel, Viv worries about paying to stay here. While she has the funds, thoughts of handing over all that coinage in the morning make her redden in anticipation. She'll look like she's robbed a piggy bank, thanks to all change from Chinese takeaways over the preceding months. Kenny spending everything she earns—plus his stipend from the government—it's been hard to scrape together the little she has. It's enough for a few nights in a genteel establishment like this, but only just.

She hopes it's not so genteel they'll balk at a single woman checking in at nine on a Friday night. Even though it's 1980 and women's rights have come a long way since the sixties, there's still oh so far still to go in some neighbourhoods. Weirdly it appears the well-to-do neighbourhoods have farther to go than most.

2

Not since she was fresh out of teachers' training college, has Viv been this nervous. The night porter is everything you'd expect in a private hotel of this nature. He's uniformed, entitled and scary as hell. Looking at her over the top of his pince-nez glasses, she knows he's found her sub-par.

Never mind her dirty clothes are hidden by her tightly-belted coat, a woman not sporting a wedding ring, who's travelling alone and only carrying one battered suitcase, is not their usual clientele.

"A conference, you say?"

"That's right." Viv tries to sound confident, but even with this two-word reply, her voice breaks, popping up an octave and firmly labelling her a liar. Teachers are so much better at euphemisms than out-and-out lies: "Tim can be a challenging pupil and needs to remain focused in class to achieve his full potential."

Better this than the truth: "Tim is a conniving little toe-rag and the world would be a better place if you'd used a condom seven years ago."

"There are no double rooms vacant." He slams the large, dark green register closed with a finality that has Viv's shoulders drooping in defeat.

She thinks for a moment. *Oh my goodness, he thinks she needs a double because...*

Pulling herself up to her full height, Viv bristles with indignation. "I'm after a single room." Her nostrils flare, but there's nothing she can do about it. Never mind she couldn't afford a double even if one was on offer. A quick glance at the prices listed in a small gilt-frame perched on the front desk has already let her know it's a single, or nothing.

He examines her minutely before slowly re-opening the register. He then runs his finger down a worryingly large number of columns. "We do have a single available. How many nights are you staying?"

The simple question is once again loaded and as much as Viv would like to reply "one night", she knows she can't. "I'd like to book in for the full week, please."

While she might be quaking in her boots about shelling out this much money, she has at least wiped the look of mistrust off his face. She'll be okay, so long as he doesn't demand payment upfront.

Viv doesn't relax until she's safely in her room under the eaves. To call the room a single is generous; she suspects the hostelry term for it is demi-chambre. Despite it being the cheapest on offer, she's honestly been expecting something larger than this glorified broom cupboard.

On the plus side, the single bed is neat and clean and—most attractive of all—doesn't have a drunken and snoring Kenny sprawled across it. The bathroom is along the hall. It's far enough away that she won't hear other guests using it, yet close enough it won't be a mission to use it herself.

The bathroom, much like her room, is also small and clean. She locks the door, delighted to be able to brush her teeth without gagging on the stench of Kenny's most recent bowel movement. She'd even taken to brushing her teeth at the kitchen sink to avoid that poisonous cloud.

Her bedtime routine is also different from usual. The biggest change is having her alarm clock on the bedside table rather than out in the hallway. She learned early on in her relationship with Kenny that he isn't a morning person.

Unfortunately, it took longer to realise he isn't that great in the afternoon or evening either. Peeling the tape away from the back of the alarm clock, she removes the small key stuck there. She slots it into the keyhole and turns it while thinking long and hard about what time to set the alarm.

There's bound to be a queue for the bathroom in the morning, her fellow guests keen to get on with seeing the sights. She settles for 5:00 a.m., doubting many others will be out and about this early on a Saturday. It's early even for her, but better to be washed and dressed and out of the hotel before anyone else is about.

Sleep doesn't come easily, her mind a swirling mire of worry. Will she get a job outside of teaching? Where will she live? Will Kenny find her?

Scant hours later, her alarm clock bellows its way to life, like a newborn, only louder. Exhausted, her eyes gritty, Viv wants to do nothing more than slam her hand on top of the clock, roll over and go back to sleep. Unfortunately, it's not a luxury she can indulge in.

Throwing back the covers, she's on her feet before her body's ready for it abd forced to put a hand against the wall in order to remain upright. All too rapidly, her worries reacquaint themselves with the pit of her stomach and any hesitation on her part is burned away with acid.

Following a quick flannel wash, Viv dons her outfit from the night before. Even though it's grubby, it's better than most of her op shop finds. Until she's had time to visit a laundromat to rid them of the smell of mothballs, these are strictly off limits.

Viv scurries through Reception, without slowing. Dropping her key on the front desk she determinedly avoids eye contact with the night porter. Anything is better than him grilling her as to why she's out and about so early on a Saturday morning.

Not far from the hotel, she spots a red pillar box. Stopping next to it, she drags the bundle of letters out of her handbag and sorts through them. She then posts letters to the few friends who've stuck by her and even the local police station. This way if Kenny does report her missing—when he runs out of food or money—the police will know she doesn't want to be found.

The final letter she posts is to her mother in Edinburgh. Better to explain everything in a letter than phone her up and be stuck with ten minutes of "I told you he was a bad egg." The letter will also be the first contact with her mum in over two years.

The decline in their relationship had been gradual and mostly due in part to Kenny considering Viv's mum to be an 'interfering old biddy'. He'd been right of course, with her mum stressing all his bad points and urging her to come home as a sign off to every phone call.

It wasn't that Kenny was privy to these conversations, but rather that he'd use any excuse to isolate Viv, the better to control her. She can see that now, of course and so doesn't need her mum pointing it out in excruciating detail.

The last letter she holds is for the headmistress of her school. There's no stamp on the envelope because some news is better delivered in person, or at least faster than the Royal Mail is capable of. If she posts it, the letter won't get there until Tuesday at the soonest.

Being as it's far too early to call on Mrs Gregory, Viv's next priority is breakfast. Even though this is on offer at the hotel, a quick scan of the inflated prices had effectively killed her appetite.

Smarter to jump on the tube and head through to a suburb that's both well away from the hotel and her old neighbourhood. She's on the lookout for a greasy spoon offering a breakfast that's large and cheap. Hopefully big enough she won't need to worry about lunch.

A couple of hours and Viv is replete, albeit greasy. A quick glance at the grimy clock hanging precariously above the deep-fryer and she knows she needs to get a move on. How long will it take to get the tube to the other side of London and find

Mrs Gregory's house? Not as long as she'd like with the reason for her visit being to break the news she won't be at school on Monday.

Nine on a Saturday morning is a respectable hour to visit, isn't it?

Before she can do that, she'll need to find a toilet. The two large mugs of tea she's taken her time sipping, have hit her bladder and started to trickle south. Thoughts of facing her headmistress with a full bladder have her fidgeting like a five-year-old who's forgotten to pee during recess.

Viv's hand hovers over the door knocker. *Maybe I should just shove the letter through the slot and run? It's not as if Mrs Gregory is at her best during the week, never mind on a Saturday morning.* She's still dithering when the door's opened.

"Miss Morgan?" Mrs Gregory's tone says it all.

Suitably reprimanded, Viv has trouble saying the words she's rehearsed over-and-over on the tube ride here. "I ah, ah was going to send you a letter, but ah, thought it better to deliver it myself."

It's only when she hears crinkling that Viv's aware she's taken the letter out of her handbag.

Mrs Gregory holds her hand out, beckoning for Viv to hand the missive over. Deciding this will be easier than speaking, Viv complies.

Rather than invite Viv into the house as would be polite, Mrs Gregory leaves her standing on the front step. Unable to face the headmistress when she reads the letter, Viv turns sideways to look at the garden. A gnome sits proudly with his fishing rod, amid regimentally planted roses. She doubts this is Mrs Gregory's work.

What's Mr Gregory like.

Spluttering from beside her apprises Viv that Mrs Gregory has got to the meat of the letter.

"But… you can't do this!" Mrs Gregory slaps the letter against her free hand, doing some crinkling of her own.

"I don't want to. I have too." Seeing her words fall on deaf ears, Viv's hands go to the collar of her high-necked blouse.

She's undone a good half-dozen buttons and spread her collar wide before Mrs Gregory rockets from annoyed and confused, to furious.

At first, Viv thinks the anger is directed at her. Only when the headmistress speaks does she understand.

"You'd better come in." This is reinforced by the older woman standing to the side and indicating Viv should lead the way. "Straight down the hall. We're in the conservatory."

We? Viv would prefer not to have an audience for this particular conversation.

Stopping just inside the glass room tacked onto the back of the house, Viv's senses are overwhelmed both by the perfume and colour. So varied and spectacular are the orchids perched on every flat surface that it takes her a second to spot the man slouched in a wicker chair, reading a paper.

"Norman, would you be as kind as to make another pot of tea?"

He lowers the paper and his gaze travels from Mrs Gregory over to Viv. She knows the moment he spots the bruises around her neck. He doesn't say anything, rather his eyebrows raise and he shakes his head slowly.

After folding the paper carefully and popping in into the cane magazine rack next to his chair, he slowly gets to his feet.

His patting Viv gently on the shoulder as he passes is her undoing, taking them all by surprise, especially Viv. She never loses it like this, knowing if she gave into a case of the 'vapours' around Kenny, she'd regret it.

Even more astounding is Mrs Gregory pulling Viv in for a tight, if slightly awkward, hug. This is a side of the headmistress Viv hasn't seen before, with the woman's reputation as a right harridan, extending well beyond the school gates and for good reason.

Spilling her guts is cathartic, albeit humiliating. It doesn't come easy with Mrs Gregory having to prod her on exactly what happened. Only then does Viv admit the abuse has been going on for years and escalating of late.

It's this revelation that has Mrs Gregory insisting she take a sabbatical through to the middle of the first term in the New Year. "Enough time for you to sort things out and avoid that odious man tracking you down."

It's more than Viv could have hoped for and she spends a lot of time on the tube ride back to the hotel shaking her head in disbelief. Sure she knows part of the reason Mrs Gregory has suggested a break is that she doesn't want Kenny hanging around the school.

"Who cares why, I'll take it," Viv whispers to herself. At least she can cross this off her list of worries. Far better her having a sabbatical listed on her CV than abandonment of post. A black mark if ever there was one.

Her main hurdle now is finding a temporary job, plus room and board until the middle of the first term after Christmas; long enough for Kenny to give up and move onto another meal ticket.

As the tube pulls into the next station, Viv stares vacantly at the advertisements for all things Christmas that pepper the curved wall that backs the platform. Her eyes widen on the realisation of how different this festive season will be. For the first time in years she won't have to watch Kenny stuffing himself, in between demands for more gravy and belching loudly enough to drown out the Christmas carols.

As the one responsible for all the cooking and the clean-up after, Viv loves the idea of spending this special day alone. Better this than slaving away in the kitchen for hours while his useless mother does nothing but sit around demanding more bottles of stout.

Viv smiles genuinely for the first time in a long time.

She's still smiling when she walks up the front steps of the genteel hotel.

"Someone's looking happy."

Viv's taken aback at how friendly the day porter is in comparison with his night-time counterpart.

"Ah, yes, I am. May I have the key to room 17, please?"

"Who on earth put you up…" The rest of the sentence stays put in his mouth. "We've got a nice double available on the first floor, if you prefer?"

Viv doesn't need to think long on this. While her tiny room on the top floor might not be the most salubrious on offer, it is the cheapest. "No, I love that room. The view over the rooftops is wonderful."

She knows she's been convincing enough

when he hands the key over without another word.

The key safely tucked in the pocket of her coat, Viv heads towards the stairs. While there is an elevator, it's one of those glorified bird cages dating back to the 1920s and would be more at home in a museum than a hotel. Unfortunately as an exhibit.

Without her suitcase to weight her down, Viv's preference is to take the stairs. Before she can put her foot on the first step, she has a thought. Turning back towards Reception, she looks around for a phone, eventually seeing one in a half-booth at the back of the foyer.

"Do you have a Yellow Pages available?" His look of astonishment tells her this isn't a common request in these parts.

"Yes, we do. Somewhere."

He disappears beneath the counter and Viv hears things shuffled left and right with the occasional bump against the polished mahogany that fronts the unit.

"Aha. Here we are." He slaps the yellow directory on top of the counter, its front cover sporting a serious layer of dust. "Just a mo." He pulls a feather duster out and flicks it ineffectually over the cover before sliding it over the counter in Viv's direction.

Up in her room, she puts her large handbag on the bed and retrieves the snacks she purchased on the way home. It's not cordon bleu, but it will be a lot cheaper than eating in the dining room downstairs. While her room is small, she's glad it has tea and coffee-making facilities.

A quick trip to the bathroom to fill the jug and she settles in for some light research and a cuppa. Flipping the large, yellow directory open to 'Employment Agencies', she runs her finger down the columns, reading each of the small ads in turn. She's trawled through several pages before an ad jumps out.

Experience with children?

Tick.

Available for immediate start?

Tick.

Live-in positions available.

Tick.

Rummaging around in her handbag, Viv locates her small notebook. She slides the gold pen that sits snugly in the spine free, and makes a note of the name and address of the agency. It's nearby, she's just not exactly sure where. Thank goodness for the London A-Z. A quick look through its dog-eared pages and she knows where she's going first thing on Monday morning.

All that's left to do now is decide how to spend the rest of her weekend. It's the first in ages that she won't be laden down with housework courtesy of first hosting and then tidying up after

Kenny's usual Saturday night session with the boys.

One thing she needs to do is visit a laundromat, even if she has to wear everything she owns in order to get past the front desk without looking likes she's doing a runner.

3

The alarm rattles to life at five on Monday morning and Viv rolls over, wishing she could go back to sleep for a couple of hours. Slamming her hand on top of it, she puts it out of *her* misery.

Rubbing her eyes goes some way towards clearing her view of the room. Her interview outfit is hanging from a hook on the back of the door; everything else remains neatly folded in her suitcase.

The outfit she's picked for her visit to the agency screams governess and so should be acceptable. It's not as though she has a lot of options.

The other thing she doesn't have much choice about is breakfast. It will be the same as dinner last night, consisting of heavy-duty rye bread with cheddar. It's filling, but not even close to appetising.

Hearing movement in the room next to hers, Viv bounds out of bed while stuffing her feet into her slippers and dragging on her dressing gown. There's no way she wants to miss first dibs in the bathroom.

She hurries down the hall with her vanity bag mere seconds later. In her haste, she'd come close to shutting the door before realising she didn't have her key with her. The last thing she wants is to have to trail downstairs to reception to get a duplicate, dressed in her nightie.

Her ablutions are efficient. The bath, being as big as it is, if she were to fill it, it would drain every hot-water cylinder in the hotel if not the entire block. She's not about to incur the wrath of her fellow guests by doing so.

A mere two inches of water in the bottom of the bath, Viv gets in and kneels rather than sit. The cast-iron is still chilly to the touch and none to gentle on her bruised knees. She flannels all over, cleaning herself as best she can. She can't afford to take too long, with her teeth chattering thanks to the rapidly cooling water.

She's brushing her teeth when she hears boards creaking out in the hallway. When the bathroom door handle rattles urgently, Viv gets enough of a fright to jab the inside of her cheek with the toothbrush. Making short work of spitting out the toothpaste, Viv rinses her mouth and wipes the basin, before collecting her belongings and making a hasty exit.

The flinty gaze of an elderly woman who clearly thinks Viv has stolen 'her spot' escorts her all the way back to her room.

"With qualifications like these, why are you interested in the sort of positions we have advertised?"

Viv's been expecting this, her answer well thought out and rehearsed with Mrs. Gregory. "I'm working on a dissertation regarding the use of one-on-one tuition in the modern schoolroom. It's something I can't do while teaching full time."

"Your reference from your current principal is glowing. We'll need to ring for confirmation that it's authentic."

"Certainly," says Viv, smiling, "the phone number is on the school letterhead." Viv was surprised Mrs Gregory had gone to the trouble of writing her a reference. And one completed in longhand on school stationery at that. All of this to a background of Mr Gregory bustling around in the kitchen, making a second cup of tea. Now she's glad of it.

"Excuse me." Leaving Viv sitting there like a common criminal, the women exits the glass-fronted office to use a phone in another similarly public space. Viv's glad not to have to sit quietly by listening to a conversation where her integrity is called into question. She almost feels sorry for the woman doing so with Mrs Gregory.

The agency rep returns, her tail between her legs. She must have got both barrels from the headmistress.

"Everything's in order. Unfortunately, we don't have anything on the books at present, but we will keep you on the top of the pile for the next available position."

Viv fights to keep her spine stiff and her shoulders back. This is not what she expected, given the desperation of their advertisement. The way it's written, she anticipated the agency staff would be fighting over her, not showing her the door. Out on the footpath, she dithers. Should she go left or right? Maybe there's a Post Office nearby where she can look at the Yellow Pages again to see if there's another agency in the area?

"Miss Morgan, a word if you will?"

Viv spins to find another of the agency's staff, head poking out of the door, eyebrows raised in question.

"Yes, of course." Viv follows the woman back inside and through to an office at the rear of the agency. She hasn't even settled herself into the offered seat before the woman outlines a position that sounds perfect. Perhaps too good to be true.

"You'll have one charge. It's live-in, but you will need to start tomorrow."

"Can you tell me more about the position? Exactly where would I be living?"

"Ah." The woman flips through a folder that's full to bursting only finding what she's after at the very back. "Ah, it's in Chelsea, I think," she says, doubt evident in her reply.

Viv scrutinises the woman. It's as if this is the first time the agency staffer has seen this particular folder, strange given the sheer size of the thing. She's no closer to a conclusion when the woman upends the wodge of paper so she can read the cover sheet. That she reads the description line-for-line, again reinforcing her unfamiliarity with the position.

"You'll be looking after one boy, Quincy, plus there are some light housekeeping duties to perform." She peers at the file again, before quickly adding. "Nothing too strenuous."

Viv doesn't have any choice. "Will the interview be this afternoon?"

"No need for that. We'll start you on a temporary basis and if Mrs Harrow is happy with your performance, you may stay on."

"That sounds wonderful." Although Viv's response is positive, she smells something fishy. If she were the boy's mother, she wouldn't want some random person turning up to take care of him. Maybe the mother's as desperate as she is.

Viv leaves the agency with the paperwork completed, the address to report to the following morning tucked safely in her handbag. A quick shufty at her watch confirms it's not even ten o'clock. If she hurries, she can catch up with them. It's also close enough she can walk rather than take a bus or the tube.

She hears the kids before she sees them, their high-pitched chatter bouncing off the walls in the Museum of London. Rounding the corner, Viv is horrified to see a lot of sticky fingers touching display cases. The museum will need to invest in Windolene stocks to put things to rights after they leave.

Clapping her hands loudly ensures she has everyone's attention before she speaks. "Children, what have I told you about not touching the glass."

"Oooh, oooh." A small hand shoots up at the back of the gaggle of children.

"Yes, Christine?"

"Not to, miss."

Viv raises an eyebrow which is enough to have small sticky fingers pulled sharply away from what had earlier, more than likely, been pristine glass. Where on earth is the teacher Mrs Gregory's put in charge of them?

Viv had been so relieved on leaving the headmistress' home the morning after her escape to know the field trip would still be going ahead as planned, even without her in attendance.

A quick scan of the room and she spots Gareth Jones slumped on a bench towards the back of the exhibit hall. He doesn't look happy. Whether it's because he's missed out on Albert's curry lunch or that he's been roped in to look after her rambunctious charges is anyone's guess.

So lost is he in his misery that he doesn't even know she's there until she speaks.

"You look like you could do with some help."

The transformation is immediate and breathtaking. Getting to his feet, he stands tall, sucks in his small paunch and a wide smile splits his face. His "Oh, thank God!" is heartfelt.

Viv can't help smiling in response.

"Does this mean you're staying on at the school?"

Her hand strays to the scarf at her throat before she says, "I can't." She'd like to say more but worries it will have her in tears. It's not a state she wants to be in when around her students, even if they're technically not hers anymore, at least not until the New Year.

His smile falters and he sucks in some air confirming he's not going to let her away with saying nothing.

She doesn't give him a chance to speak, holding her hand up like a policeman on traffic duty. Shaking her head, she turns and flees in the direction of the children where she knows conversation will be impossible.

The rest of the morning is spent answering questions of a historic nature and avoiding Gareth at every turn. The plan for lunch is to spend it in the gardens that huddle next to the remains of the Roman wall that once enclosed the original City of London. After this, there'll be a quick look at the Barbican Centre and then home. For once the weather is on their side, although the closer they get to midday, the more Viv notices Albert fidgeting, his lunch anxiety on full alert.

Seeing him splitting away from the group to check out a cabinet crammed full of old Roman coins, Viv sidles up next to him. She reaches into her large handbag and pulls out a plastic bag, passing it over without a word.

Never have two bits of white bread, some chicken and limp tomato received such unspoken praise. His head lifts and he beams before returning to join his classmates. The small boy has a spring in his step.

"You love them, don't you?"

Viv spins to find Gareth closer than she'd like, his expression is one of bemusement.

Wandering away, she throws "What's not to love?" nonchalantly over her shoulder before being eagerly swallowed up by 'her kids'.

. . .

"Harry, if I see you throwing any more pickled onions, I'm going to be exceedingly cross." Viv holds onto her stern expression, although only just, with her laughter fighting for supremacy.

She's thankful lunch is being eaten outside, with Harry and three of his mates deciding the lunches packed by their mums are better used in the re-creation of a Roman battle. By comparison, Albert has savoured every mouthful of the sandwich Viv purchased for him after she finished at the employment agency.

Much as she tried to avoid it, Gareth has scoped out a spot right next to her on a bench sitting hard against the remains of the Roman wall. Leaning back, Viv enjoys the heat of the sun that's stored in the stone, seeping through her coat.

Unable to make her sandwich last any longer, Viv pops the last piece of bread into her mouth and screws up the wrappings. This time, Gareth isn't having a bar of it.

"The Old Dragon said you were on a leave-of-absence. You want to tell me why you didn't mention it on Friday?"

Damn, she should never have joined them here. If it'd been any of the other teachers covering for her, she'd be okay, but she and Gareth go back a long way, having gone to teachers' training college together.

They'd even dated for a short time, just long

enough to end up in the sack together after one particularly riotous pub crawl. A night shrouded in mystery for Viv due to an afternoon of drinking games.

"I've been having, ah, trouble at home."

He turns sideways on the bench so that he can look at her properly. Viv, however, keeps staring straight ahead to avoid eye contact. If she looks at him, she'll lose it.

"It's that bastard Kenny, isn't it?"

"Language, Gareth," says Viv.

"Well, you give me a better title, then."

Viv can think of several, but she's not sharing those with Gareth. Settling back against the wall, Viv closes her eyes to the sun, hoping Gareth will leave her alone. She didn't sleep well last night and now she's fighting to keep her eyes open. Maybe it's because it's so warm. Unbuttoning her coat helps, removing her scarf even more so.

That is, until she hears the sharp intake of breath from Gareth, still sitting beside her on the bench. Damn, she forgot about the bruises on her neck.

4

Even on the tube with Gareth and the full complement of children, a herculean task in its own right, he's not letting it go. He continues to badger her about what the hell went on at the weekend and why she hasn't gone to the police.

Viv doesn't bother explaining that going to the police is the last thing she can do. They'd be more likely to tell her she's lucky to have a bloke and to go home and cook him some dinner. In the eyes of many of the old guard, she's nothing but a chattel. Thank goodness Mrs Gregory burned a few bras in her younger years.

She resorts to putting her fingers in her ears until he finally gives up. It's childish, but it works.

By then it's too late.

He's distracted her and she's forgotten to get off at the station closest to the hotel. She's now far closer to her old domicile than she'd like to be and in real danger of running into Kenny.

How real becomes apparent when the tube pulls into the station closest to the school and Viv spots Kenny at the same time as he sees her. Even with the tube still moving and solid glass between them, she can tell he's calling her every name under the sun.

"Shit, that's not good."

So shocked is Viv by Kenny's proximity she doesn't even think to reprimand her fellow teacher on his language. She knows his oath has been loud enough for the kids to hear with the most boisterous of them crowing in a singsong chant. "Oooooh, Mr Jones said SHIT!" with their emphasis on the bad word.

The tube is still moving when Kenny runs alongside their carriage, already worming his fingers between the rubber stoppers where the sliding doors meet. Gareth jumps to his feet and places himself in the middle of the aisle between Viv and her ex.

He bounces on his feet, fists already up in a fighting stance. "Harry! You got any of those pickled onions left?" he yells over his shoulder.

Viv has no idea what Gareth's on about asking such a random question. Harry, however, understands, immediately pulling a half-full jar of the noxious snack from his haversack and holding it up like a trophy. Beside him, his mates are busy arming themselves with apple cores and half-eaten sandwiches.

Having removed the lid from his jar of pickled onions, Harry looks to Gareth for direction. "The geezer in the Aston Villa jacket?"

"That's the one. Don't hold back!"

Shoving passengers out of his way, Kenny barges onto the carriage and is lurching in her direction when the first pickled onion hits him in the chest. This is followed closely by any item of food not deemed worthy of lunch and even a few lunch boxes.

Whether this is down to most of her students supporting local football clubs, or the chance to let loose in a public place, Viv doesn't know. As food fights go, it's epic and rather one-sided. However, it isn't an item of food that does the most to halt Kenny's progress; it's a small tartan thermos.

Viv is frozen, watching the mêlée as though in slow motion, when a small hand slides into hers. It's enough to pull her frightened gaze away briefly to see who it is. It's Albert and he looks to be as scared as she is.

"Come, Miss Morgan." Only when he tugs hard on her hand does he break through her terror. This sees her staggering to her feet and following him through the single door at the end of the carriage.

She doesn't dare look back because for such a

small boy, Albert is fast on his feet. He's also nimble and it takes every ounce of Viv's concentration to keep up with him without running into passengers heading in the opposite direction. The stairs at the end of the platform are tantalisingly close when Albert yanks on her hand and takes her through a side tunnel.

He doesn't slow and she follows him straight onto a tube heading back towards the city. They don't have time to catch their breath before the doors shut and the tube lurches forward. Looking through the windows, she gets the merest glimpse of Kenny. It's enough to see him slide his finger across his throat in a manner that tightens hers.

Unable to return to the school, there's nothing but for Viv to take Albert home, although only after he's reassured her there'll be someone there. She's still surprised when rather than be greeted at the door by Albert's mum it's his grandmother who answers. At least that's who Viv thinks she is. Only after the third or fourth polite smile does it occur to Viv that English isn't the old lady's strong suit. Despite the warm welcome, she wouldn't have a clue who Viv is, or what she's on about.

It therefore takes a while for Viv to explain to

Albert's grandmother that he isn't in trouble and that he's a good student. It's obvious the old girl isn't taking the boy's word for it when he repeats her words in whatever dialect it is they speak. Thankfully gentle patting on top of Albert's head is a universal enough sign for the old lady to accept the truth of it.

Explaining that the missing Taj-Mahal-of-lunchboxes is Viv's fault is a much bigger challenge, with even Albert struggling for the right words.

When Mrs Chaudhary Senior packs up some curry for Viv to take with her, she isn't sure if this is as a thank you for escorting Albert home or down to a dodgy translation.

The trip back to the hotel is convoluted and overly long with her eschewing the tube in favour of the bus. She sees the inside of a lot of them and has even pounded the pavements before she staggers into the hotel.

Getting past reception with the lunchbox full of reeking curried goodness is only achieved by wrapping her coat around the thing. She then makes sure she gets the key to her room before the receptionist gets a whiff of Albert's gran's cooking.

The food and even her tiny room on the top floor are welcome after thc day she's had. It's not even eight before she's enjoyed a curry that's stupendous, even cold and a bath—also cold. After a couple of hours working on a tentative lesson plan, she switches off the light in hopes of a decent night's sleep. If today was big, tomorrow promises to be huge.

The last thing she thinks about before falling asleep is the letter she'd penned on the back of a Chinese takeout menu Mrs Chaudhary had given her. This was handed to Albert for him to deliver to Gareth at school the next day.

Viv finds the Harrow residence easily enough the next morning. It's her first time in what turns out to be Belgravia rather than Chelsea. Mrs Harrow lives in a multi-dwelling building which is something of a surprise.

There's nothing sub-standard about the building, its swathes of red brick and soft grey stone, are high-end through and through. It's more that with an active child in the house, Viv's been expecting a larger establishment, one with some outside space for him to run around and play.

Viv checks the note given to her by the agency once more to be sure it's the right place, before walking up the front steps and between the imposing columns that frame the entrance. She drops her suitcase on the ornately tiled top step and pushes the single doorbell that sits to the right of the front door. She then waits, although not for long.

"Hah, you the latest, then?" a man's voice says from beside her but below ground level. "Name's Jack. Be with you in a tick."

True to his word, the front door opens a moment later and he swings it wide to allow her to enter. She's in front of the elevator doors at the back of the foyer when there's a discreet cough from behind. The doorman stands next to a narrow door off to the side, his waggling eyebrows indicating it's where she should be going.

Servant's entrance it is, then.

This sees her following him down a set of narrow stairs and through a rabbit warren of even narrower passages. A bigger woman than she would be pushed to make her way through some gaps. As it is Viv has to hold her suitcase out awkwardly in front because it wouldn't fit beside her without catching on the multitude of pipes that dot the passages.

Inexorably they make their way to what feels like the next block over before he stops next to a set of elevator doors. These are utilitarian compared with their public-facing counterparts.

Viv's standing at the back of the large, obviously freight, elevator, when the doorman leans in, pushes the '6' button and pulls back out again.

"Aren't you coming with me?"

"'ell no. Mrs Dunning, the 'ousekeeper, would

'and me my balls in a bag if I was ta access the private quarters."

As slow as the doors have been to close, the elevator is even slower. So slow in fact, it takes a moment for Viv to realise she's even on her way up. It does, however, give her time to work on settling her nerves.

Licking her index finger, she first sweeps it first across one eyebrow and then the other. Patting the bun on the back of her head, she checks for loose hairs, before straightening her already-straight skirt. All of this is done by feel. There aren't any mirrors in the beast she's travelling in and its metal walls are so dinged and scraped as to kill off any reflections.

Even though she's expecting it, she's still surprised when the doors open straight onto a small service area. She's even able to see into the kitchen of the apartment through an open door opposite the elevator.

The doors haven't had time to death-rattle their way shut before a large woman storms out of the kitchen. She throws an autocratic "follow me" at Viv and disappears through another door, leaving Viv scrambling to follow.

If she didn't know the matron from her old boarding school to be long dead, Viv would swear she's following Miss Cabot. Hard military bearing, steel-grey hair, face like a baboon's arse? Yep, it's all there. Here's hoping the woman doesn't also prove herself to be an out-and-out cow of the first order.

"In here." The woman, who can only be Mrs Dunning, the doorman's nemesis, slams her hand hard against the door she's standing next to. This reveals a room as neat as a pin and about the same size, making the demi-chambre at the hotel look palatial by comparison. Viv inches her way in and drops her suitcase next to the bed, all while eyeing the battleship grey uniform laid on the counterpane.

Viv is both relieved and dismayed. Relieved she doesn't need to worry about the meagre contents of her small suitcase being up to snuff. Dismayed that the uniform looks to be one of the housekeeper's cast-offs. She will swim in it. Thankfully, it's something Mrs Dunning sees.

After a masculine-sounding "*Hummpf*", she leaves Viv on her own. But not without telling her to "Wait!" is a tone more commonly used at dog obedience classes. It's as though Viv is a Scottish terrier rather than simply Scottish.

The woman takes her time returning, leaving Viv unsure of herself. *Should she unpack or is she meant to start work immediately?* It's already gone nine and so any charge of hers should already be at their lessons.

Viv still thinks it's off that a seven-year-old isn't enrolled at one of the up-market schools in this area of London. Or failing that bundled up and sent to a prep school in readiness for Eton or Cambridge.

Uncertainty is wiggling its way under the skin of her psyche before Mrs Dunning returns with another uniform. This one is closer to Viv's size and the grey less gunnery sergeant in hue.

"Once you've changed, make your way to the kitchen along the hall and I'll brief you on your 'other' duties."

Viv is alone before she notices the older woman's stress on the word 'other'. Nothing she can't handle.

It's a sentiment she revises, when on walking into the kitchen in her uniform. Mrs Dunning hands her a rubber apron and nods at what looks like a dinner party's worth of washing up. A large dinner party.

A VERY LARGE dinner party.

Light housekeeping duties my bum.

"Oh, I thought I'd need to start young Quincy's lessons by now?"

"Hah, right. No, he and 'her ladyship' will still be abed until at least eleven."

Viv analyses this seemingly simple statement while running hot water into a sink large enough to bathe a baby. Horse.

What did Mrs Dunning mean? It isn't so much what she said as how she said it.

So far as Viv is aware her new employer isn't

titled, with the woman at the employment agency referring to her simply as Mrs Harrow.

While a title wouldn't be uncommon in this neighbourhood, the way Mrs Dunning said 'her ladyship' implies this is self-imposed rather than the real deal. There's also the fact a seven-year-old boy is allowed to lay abed until eleven on a school day. Even if he's home-schooled, it's not healthy.

It takes Viv an hour to clear the kitchen bench of dirty dishes, dry them and, through trial and error, put everything away. By her estimations, there had to have been at least twenty people at dinner the night before. Thankfully all the dishes had been rinsed before they were stacked or her task would have been even more onerous.

She's barely hung the rubber apron on a hook next to the door that, presumably, leads to Mrs Harrow's quarters, before Mrs Dunning speaks again. Not that the woman is verbose, by any means.

No, she hands Viv a bucket full of cleaning equipment, the word "Come" tossed carelessly in her direction. There's nothing but to follow the woman along a narrow hallway and through a swinging door and to be smart about it for fear of losing her guide.

Their destination is a bathroom larger than

the front room at the terrace house she'd shared with Kenny.

"I'll be back in half an hour and I expect it to be clean enough to eat off. If it's not, your trial is over."

And this, right here explains why that file at the employment agency is as fat as it is.

5

Viv isn't sure whether Mrs Dunning is referring to the floor, the bath or the toilet when it comes to porcelain suitable for culinary purposes. Either way, she doesn't waste time getting stuck in.

Who'd have thought all those years of trying desperately to keep Kenny happy would come in handy? Still, better to be slaving away in solitude, than doing it to a background of Kenny telling her to hurry up because he needed to take a dump.

She'd once suggested he might like to do this before she cleaned the toilet. It was something that saw him shove her so far down the bowl that her face was worryingly close to the water.

Sadly not so far that she didn't hear, "Would you want your arse near that mess?" The irony that the skid marks in question were courtesy of his poisoned digestive tract had been lost on him. Or maybe not.

Viv is finishing the mirror when Mrs Dunning returns. The place sparkles enough that Kenny wouldn't think twice about relieving himself here. Viv is confident it will also pass the culinary purposes test of her new boss. While Mrs Harrow might technically be her employer, Viv's under no illusions as to who calls the shots.

Again all she secures is a "*Hummpf*" and the bucket being snatched from her hand. This then being dumped unceremoniously behind the door suggests Viv is up to snuff. This is doubly confirmed when Mrs Dunning says "I'll take you through to meet Lady Harrow."

Interesting, her new boss does carry a title. Viv crosses her fingers the woman isn't as entitled as some nobility are, considering themselves well above the likes of her.

Viv again follows Mrs Dunning as best she can. Seeing how far along the parqueted hall her boss has gone, Viv trots to catch up. She's close on Mrs Dunning's heels when the woman swerves through the last door on the left.

The only occupant in the ornately Georgian room is a softly-rounded woman sitting on a straight-backed seat, upholstered in a self-stripe gold fabric. She looks to be crowding eighty, so there's no way she can be mother to a seven-year-old. Even in retrospect, her ovaries would have been like shrivelled raisins at the beginning of the gestation period. *Maybe the wee chap is adopted.*

It takes Viv a second to see Lady Harrow isn't alone after all. A small, and unnaturally blue, poodle is curled up next to her.

"You may take my darling for his morning constitutional now." Lady Harrow leans over and kisses the small dog on top of his head and Viv's wiped her mouth with the back of her hand before she's conscious of doing so. Brought up to think of dogs as dirty creatures, seeing someone choosing to put their mouth this close to one, sets her stomach roiling.

That Lady Harrow then flips the mutt onto his back and peppers his tummy with more kisses has Viv close to gagging. The aristocratic old girl is a circumcision away from going down on the dog.

It takes Viv a second to see the diamante-studded lead Mrs Dunning is dangling in front of her face. It's a moment longer before she understands she's not going to meet her charge just yet. Most kids would be bouncing off the walls by this time of day, never mind still in bed.

Out in the hall with the blue dog under her control, Viv is escorted to the front door by the housekeeper. Typical. The dog has better access privileges than she does.

"The key to the park is on the leash. I'd suggest you hurry unless you're keen on cleaning poodle piddle off the parquet."

Viv's out in the foyer before she's able to find the words she's looking for. "Ah, when will I get to meet young Quincy?"

Mrs Dunning doesn't bother responding other than to glare at Viv and then slam the front door in her face.

"Well, that's rich," says Viv to the empty foyer, although the poodle does look up at her, his expression saying he agrees.

She's never been in charge of a dog before and isn't sure of the protocol. At the very least she's undoubtedly supposed to know his name if she's to call him when he's off the lead. *Should she even do that?*

Being careful to avoid actually touching the dog, Viv twists his collar around until she's able to read his name tag.

"What!?"

She's being paid fifty quid a week plus board and lodging to take a poodle out to pee in a park? *So much for all my lovely lesson plans.*

Viv settles in over the next month, worked to the bone by Mrs Dunning, who doesn't appear to do anything but cook meals. And, there's not much work involved in these either, with them being distinctly lacklustre to appeal to Lady Harrow's limited palate.

Viv is also responsible for greeting all guests at the front door, given the housekeeper's 'old bones' aren't up to hurrying. She can't complain; the work is easier than putting up with Kenny. And because she doesn't leave the apartment, other than to take Quincy out for his thrice-daily constitutionals, she's managing to save more in one month than she had in the previous six. That her wages are paid in notes that smell strongly of mothballs also means she gets to keep it all with Lady Harrow not bothering about anything so trifling as tax.

It'd all be great if it wasn't for Rupert, Lady Harrow's nephew. He's the wrong side of both forty years and fourteen stone, balding and has personality quirks most commonly seen in locked wards. His biggest delusion is the one about his artistic talent.

Unfortunately, it's a delusion shared by Lady Harrow. This sees Viv stuck with dusting an assortment of paintings she'd grudgingly award a single gold star and then only out of sympathy for the student responsible.

Dusting his amateur paintings is the least of her worries when it comes to the honourable Rupert Smythe-Brown. No, as luck would have it, he's also got the remnants of a British public school education. Namely, a longing to be deemed naughty enough to have his bottom paddled, 'til pink and preferably by someone with the bearing of Mrs Dunning.

Before Viv knew this, she caught Rupert looking in her direction and had glared at him using her best schoolmistress mien. A pity then that grumpy schoolteacher is like catnip to this particular member of London the slap and tickle set.

Now, if she hears his voice or gets a whiff of the cloying aftershave he bathes in, she's off to the farthest reaches of the apartment. And if he tracks her down, she's fully prepared to spray herself with enough furniture polish that he won't be able to get a good grip.

Hearing a firm knock at the front door, Viv can tell it's not Rupert. The *rat-ta-tat* is too forceful and given his preferred-nephew status, he has a key.

Viv opens the front door and is faced with two young women who look to be in their mid-twenties. Next to them stands Jack, the odious doorman who haunts the downstairs foyer as though it's a bridge to his troll.

Because there's nothing in the book about visitors today, Viv keeps her welcome on the chilly side of reserved and is pleased to see the visitors' chirpiness wilt. This does nothing to shut them up though, with the blonde wittering on about a coat for Quincy.

So ludicrous is this notion Viv's about to give them the heave-ho when Lady Harrow trills out that she's been expecting them. Good of the old girl to tell her staff about it.

Viv shows the visitors to the drawing room; all while imagining Quincy decked out in a canine version of something from Saville Row. It's about as ludicrous as her students turning up to class in high-end formal wear.

Leaving the visitors—who aren't offered refreshments—with Lady Harrow, Viv goes in search of some morning tea. She's down to dregs and crumbs when the drawing room bell rings, announcing the doggie tailors are ready to leave.

She's glad their visit hasn't been too long as it's time for her and Quincy to go to the park in the middle of the Square. Viv now looks forward to these outings, liking the fresh air after the over-heated stuffiness of the apartment and a chance to be alone with her thoughts.

Timing is also critical if she's to avoid the perfectly alliterated 'poodle pee on the parquet'. Cleaning it up would have her far closer to a dog's private parts than she would ever want to be.

Having overhead the young visitors talking about the elevator playing up, Viv collects Quincy from the drawing room. There's no way she's going to risk getting stuck like they were. After a show of opening and shutting the front door, she sneaks him through to the back of the apartment and into the service elevator. Better to risk Lady Harrow's wrath than be stuck in the elevator-equivalent of an upright freezer with a dog that's bladder is full to the brim.

Something that's blissfully empty is the park itself, with none of the other regular dog walkers in attendance. It's just her, the barren winter landscape and a blue poodle. That is until Viv hears her name shouted.

This isn't good.

No one around here knows her name other than Mrs Dunning, Lady Harrow and Jack the doorman. The voice doesn't belong to any of them.

Spinning, Viv slips off the edge of the narrow path, landing heavily on her knees. She crouches down even further, hidden by a small brick wall. She's safe for now but effectively trapped in the private park.

It's been over a month since she escaped and with his lack of energy, she thought Kenny would have given up trying to track her down by now. As to how he's found her here, she doesn't have a clue. On a more positive note, he can't get to her without a key to the wrought iron gate that ensures the park stays private to the Square's residents.

There's not a chance he can scale the chest-height fence. At least, not without catching his gut or a goolie on one of the spikes that guard the top as assiduously as a Rottweiler with a bad tooth.

The cold is seeping into her bones before she hears her name again, this time from right behind her, in a hoarse whisper. Flailing around, relief floods through her to see it's Gareth. That Quincy rushes over to stand between her and her fellow teacher is the biggest surprise.

Do toy breeds even do this? Isn't this sort of protective behaviour the predilection of the bruiser classes?

Gareth takes a big step back and Viv realises the bark end must look a whole lot more intimidating than the end that's worryingly close to her face. It takes a moment for her to understand what's happening.

It's so blasted long since she laughed; the sensation sits awkwardly on her frame. It takes hold when Gareth joins in and, as if sensing Viv is no longer in danger, Quincy joins in, barking joyously and jumping on the spot. Only when the dog trots over and sniffs Gareth's shoe does the Welshman put his hand down so the poodle can nuzzle it.

He must pass the sniff test, because Quincy is soon all over him, unfortunately, in a rather amorous fashion.

"Get a room, you two," says Viv, before dissolving into giggles again.

Gareth looks at her. “Oh, I’m sorry. Here, let me help you up.”

On her feet, Viv dusts herself as best she can. “What are you doing here? Shouldn’t you be in class?”

“I was told to get in touch with you, urgently. Because you don’t have access to a phone, I thought it best to come in person rather than write to you.”

Viv’s not surprised Gareth knows where she lives, as she’d included it in the letter she’d handed over to Albert Chaudrey all those weeks ago. This had been handed to Albert with instructions to give it to Gareth so he could in turn pass it on to the Mrs Gregory. The last thing she’s been expecting is to see him here in person.

It’s more that Mrs Gregory asked Viv to stay in touch and she didn’t have the heart to get Albert to hand a letter over to the headmistress personally. It would have been more than the small chap could cope with.

“Where’s the fire?”

“Huh? Oh, right. Your ex has been hanging around the school asking the kids if they know where you are and generally being a nuisance. Mrs Gregory wanted to make sure you didn’t give into the temptation to drop by for a visit because you were missing your kids.”

The headmistress knows Viv well, as she’s been thinking of doing this very thing on her next day off. She's missing the scruffy little tearaways like crazy. "Didn't the school call the police?"

"They did, but he's always gone by the time they arrive. We gave them your old address, but it looks like he's no longer in residence. The windows are boarded up, apparently."

Viv closes her eyes for a second before they snap open again. There isn't a chance Kenny will have moved on, with that involving far too much effort on his part. More likely he's stopped paying rent and the landlord has boarded the place up in an attempt to stop him from squatting.

Despite being a lazy bastard, there's no way a few boards would stop Kenny from getting in. Especially not when his living there rent-free would mean he can spend the entirety of his benefit on beer and takeaways.

Viv knows for sure his mum isn't gullible enough to allow him to move back in with her. The woman had been positively gleeful when Kenny and Viv moved in together all those years ago. In hindsight his mum muttering that he was her responsibility now should have been a warning.

"Hang on. What if he saw you leave in the middle of the day? He knows you know me. What if he followed you?"

Viv no longer feels like laughing. Now she

feels exposed, with a freshly painted target on her back.

"Oh, shit. I don't think he was around."

"But you can't be sure?"

"No." Gareth scans the footpaths around the edge of the Square as frantically as Viv.

A couple of full rotations confirm the Square is mercifully free of grubby, overweight, geezers. Viv worries it might not stay this way and makes short work of clipping the lead back onto Quincy's collar and dragging him over to the gate.

Gareth keeps apace with them, even accompanying them through the Mews to the back of the property. He even escorts her and Quincy inside the portico where she presses the button for the service elevator.

Although they've been vigilant about keeping an eye out for Kenny, Viv doesn't relax until she's seen Gareth disappear around the corner of the Mews and she and Quincy are in the service elevator.

She's about to push the button for the top floor when her hand stills. What if? Deciding to err on the side of caution, she presses every button so that if anyone does happen upon the back entrance to the building, they won't be able to tell on which floor she's got off at.

6

The service elevator is slow at the best of times. Stopping at every floor, it appears to take forever. Each time it stops, Quincy gets to his feet, ready to leave.

"Not yet, boy."

The dog looks at her as if she's barking, but her sixth sense has saved her from Kenny's wrath on more than one occasion. The hairs on the back of her neck being strictly at attention – it's a warning she won't ignore.

The lock on the back door downstairs will be child's play to her larcenous ex and so the elevator is the next best barrier. This way, he'll be stuck searching all the floors before he reaches the sixth. Her hope is this will give the building's other occupants plenty of opportunity to intercept him.

. . .

"You took your sweet time. Her Ladyship won't be happy to see Quincy shivering like that."

Viv hasn't been aware of the state of the dog until it's pointed out by Mrs Dunning, her own personal Sergeant Major. The woman's right though, the dog looks to be perishing.

Being responsible for an animal is a challenge compared to looking after kids. Unlike a dog, they'll tell you loudly and often what they're feeling at any second of the day, whether you want to know, or not.

"Come on, Quincy, let's get you toasty."

Normally, Viv's go-to for warming someone or something is hot water, but there's no way she's going anywhere near that immaculate poodle clip. Her luck of late will see her screw it up. No, much safer to take the pooch to her box room and turn the fan heater on full-bore. The dimensions of her private space being what they are, it'll be tropical in no time.

She watches the dog unfurl in front of the heater and it occurs to her that only a few weeks back, the thought of choosing to have the dog in her bedroom would have been anathema to her. Maybe it's that he smells better than a lot of her students and doesn't appear to shed hair at all.

Quincy is positively glowing when Viv hears a commotion in the Mews. It's not the usual clatter of deliveries or the rubbish collection and even from up here, she recognises Kenny's bastardisation of the English language.

No!

Scrambling to her feet, she sidles over to the small window until she's jammed hard up against the curtains. She looks at an oblique angle down into the small space behind the building dreading what it is she's going to see.

A quick glimpse and she jerks back. It's been enough to see Jack grasping Kenny firmly by the ear. Given the disparity in their sizes, the doorman shouldn't have been able to keep Kenny under control like this. He must have hidden skills because Kenny is howling in pain and tottering along behind Jack, his head bent to the side in an apparent attempt to keep the pressure off his lug.

Another quick gander is enough to see Kenny her lumpy ex dragged down the Mews in the direction of Eaton Place. There's no way Viv's missing out on what happens next.

"Come on, Quincy, you'll be warm enough now."

She flips the knob on top of the heater to the off position and is surprised to see the dog's shoulders visibly droop. Hah, such a human emotion from the little fur ball.

Grabbing her coat off her bed, Viv opens the door of her bedroom and is surprised at how cold the hall feels by comparison. It's something

Quincy obviously picks up on too with the amount of stalling that's going on.

"Come on, mister. It's not that bad," she says, clicking her fingers to get him moving again. If she's to see what happens to Kenny, they both need to get a wriggle on. Lucky for her, the dog is close behind her when she walks out into the hallway. Leaving him to trot to the drawing room, she nips out of the front door, opening and closing it as quietly as she can.

Racing across the foyer, she throws herself through the door that leads to the stairs, racing up them two at a time and scrambling to get the key to the door at the top from its hiding spot. Opening it, a blast of cold air takes her breath away. The park is sheltered by comparison and she had no idea it would be this polar up here. Her lack of a hat, gloves and scarf will see *her* defrosting in front of the fan heater after this escapade.

She makes it to the parapet that backs the building in time to see Jack and Kenny clear the Mews. At this point, Viv's expecting Jack to send Kenny on his way with a boot to his flabby arse. Instead the pair round the corner into Eaton Place as one and disappear from view.

Where on earth is the doorman taking him? Do they even need a police station in this neighbourhood?

Viv flies across the roof to the other side, her nose now running as fast as she is. Her hands stuffed in the pockets of her coat, her fingers curl around a long-forgotten tissue. It'll have to do.

She blows her nose and shelters behind a chimney stack, all while watching Jack and Kenny stumbling along the footpath away from the heart of Belgravia. Her vivid imagination envisages a border of sorts.

They don't get far before a black and white police car pulls up next to them. Whether this is by design or coincidence, Viv isn't sure, but Kenny is having none of it.

Yanking hard against Jack's hold on his ear, he bellows in pain, before taking off at a sprint. An officer explodes from the police car and is in pursuit seconds later.

Jack, meanwhile, dusts his hands together in the sign of a job well done, salutes the police officer still in the car and turns towards home. All the action now well out of sight, Viv wastes no time in hightailing it off the roof. She doesn't bother waiting for the world's dodgiest elevator on the sixth floor.

Instead she flies down the stairs to the ground floor in hopes of intercepting Jack. She's in luck, entering the foyer at the same time as he does, although he's nowhere near as out of breath as she is. His examination of her is clinical and then critical. "So, you're the one he was bleating on about."

"Not here." Viv's gaze darts in the direction of the door leading to the lower level.

Rather than acknowledge her request for privacy, he walks towards the door and then through it. His leaving it ajar is the only indication she's to follow him. It's an invitation he doesn't need to repeat.

Gossip that he is, Jack's spilling the beans on what's transpired with Kenny before the door's even shut properly. Jaqueline Fortescue's butler caught Kenny snooping around on the first floor and gave him into Jack's care soon after. Apparently Smithson's ex-army and there wasn't a chance Kenny was getting away from him.

"Your bloke kept saying 'e was after his fiancée, 'cause she'd stolen somethin' from 'im. I said to 'im that unless his fiancée was the wrong side of seventy, he 'ad the wrong building."

"Thank you for that."

Jack pulls himself up to his full height, a good head below Viv's own. "Didn't do it for you, love. Can't 'ave the old girls being upset by riffraff the likes of 'im skulking about."

This leaves Viv in no doubt of her place in the pecking order. "Do you think he'll come back?"

"Not a chance. Not with the local coppers being on the lookout for 'im. They might well have collared 'im already. PC Walker doesn't live up to 'is name."

It takes Viv a moment to deconstruct his sentence. She hopes he's right because it would be a huge relief to think Kenny's next domicile is Wormwood Scrubs prison. She'd be able to get back on with her life, at least for the foreseeable future.

Shame then, that the hairs on the back of her neck say this is a big, fat, no, that he's still at large and will bide his time. Waiting is something Kenny's good at when it comes to getting even. Shame he hadn't displayed the same patience where she was concerned.

Viv is vigilant over the next week, scuttling to and from the park as quickly as possible and not giving Quincy the opportunity to so much as sniff the same piece of ground twice. The quicker he does his business, the better she likes it.

Warming them both up in her room afterwards is now a regular part of their routine. It doesn't matter that the small dog is now sporting a smart new coat courtesy of Samantha, the doggie tailor. The closer they get the Christmas, the colder it gets to the point Viv wouldn't mind a new coat as warm as those Quincy now trots around in.

The other new addition to the household is a gorgeous little painting of Quincy that sits in the guest bathroom. This had been a gift to Lady Harrow from the doggie tailor's friend and a true masterpiece in miniature. It was also something Lady Harrow refused to have sitting on the mantle next to 'Rupert's works of art'.

'Works of arse', more like it.

Instead her ladyship had asked Viv to deal with it—posh talk for binning the painting—and something that had upset Jennie, the artist. Viv at first thought of hanging it in her own room, but then decided it would be better in the hall bathroom.

Here it can be seen by any guests of Lady Harrow and no doubt compared unfavourably to Rupert's daubs. Anything to show the upper crust English git in as dim light as possible is a plus in Viv's eyes.

Having expected a break by accompanying her Ladyship, Quincy and Mrs Dunning to the family's country pile for Christmas, Viv's disappointed not to be invited. Apparently, the groom at the country place takes care of Quincy's needs when he's down there, so her services won't be required.

No, Viv can keep an eye on the house and do a bit of dusting while she's about it, this last instruction courtesy of Mrs Dunning. Perhaps the biggest disappointment about not being taken to a safe place is that because her charge won't be on the premises, her wages will be halved.

Viv isn't sure if this is down to her ladyship or the penny-pinching Mrs Dunning with any savings going straight into that battle-axe's pocket. Still, Viv can't complain too much, with her accommodation still being free.

The day after her Ladyship and Mrs Dunning leave for the country Viv discovers the heating has been turned off. Whether this is by accident or as another cost-cutting exercise by the housekeeper, she's not sure. Either way the place is perishing.

"Good lord, how many layers do you have on?"

Until Gareth mentions it, Viv hasn't been aware she's done up like a strudel, although thinking back; she'd been surprised on leaving the apartment to find it as warm outside as it had been in. Or was that the other way around? Certainly the fan heater in her box room has been working overtime to stop her from freezing to death overnight.

In the warmth of the pub, Viv can't shed the layers fast enough. It's that or be overcome by the heat. Down to jeans and a sweatshirt, the bench seat on her side of the booth is now piled high with her scarf, hat, extra jumper, coat and gloves.

By comparison, there's a single coat on the seat next to Gareth.

"Lady Harrow had the heating turned off when she left for the country. At least I think it was her."

"She what!"

Viv shrugs. "Mrs Dunning told the caretaker there's no point heating the whole place for one person and to shut it down until their return."

"If it's too cold, you can always stay in the spare room at my place until she gets back."

"Gareth, we've talked about this." Viv has many reasons why she doesn't want to stay at his place, the foremost being Kenny more than likely knows where it is. She also doesn't want Gareth to get the wrong idea. Sure, university was a long time ago, but feelings don't change that much. Do they?

Gareth opens his mouth as if to press the matter, but rather than do so, he stands. "Name your poison."

"I'll have a cider, please."

"Beef or lamb for your main?"

"Beef, please," says Viv, her mouth already watering at thoughts of a full roast lunch complete with Yorkshire pudding. She looks briefly at the blackboard on the wall above the bar. Yum, the set lunch comes complete with Spotted Dick and custard for dessert.

Viv watches Gareth push his way through the

crowd towards the bar where he places the order for their Christmas lunch and drinks.

His paying doesn't sit well with Viv but neither does she want to make a scene by arguing about it. She'll make it up to him when she's back on her feet and Kenny is nothing but an unpleasant memory.

Watching her fellow teacher at the bar Viv can't help but notice how good-looking he is. She can't remember why they hadn't carried on dating back in the day. Maybe because she wanted to focus on her studies? Turning away from him to stare at their battered tabletop, she's at a loss. Maybe once she's over Kenny?

She's still deep in thought when a glass of cider appears in front of her. It's a pint glass.

"Good heavens, I won't be able to drink all that."

"Give it your best shot. It's not like we're going back to work after this."

"No, but I do want my wits about me if anything should happen." Kenny is never far from Viv's thoughts. Her neck hairs are twitching ninety to the dozen and that's never a good sign. "Have you seen any more of him?"

Gareth opens his mouth to speak, then shuts it again. His internal battle is as evident as if he were having an open punch-up with one of the other patrons.

"Spill."

"Okay, but don't freak out."

Viv's already disobeying orders.

"Yeah, well, he was following me by the time I got to the tube station ..."

"And."

"I managed to give him the slip."

"Managed or think you managed?"

"Last I saw, he was on the tube heading for Wimbledon. Short of him being able to stop the train, there's no way he could have followed me."

"What about the emergency brake? The guy's crazy enough to pull it."

"I, ah. Oh, shit."

Viv's appetite is replaced by her gut churning so hard she'd be a fool to let it anywhere near food. Without thinking, she picks up her pint of cider and gulps half-a-dozen mouthfuls. This burns its way into her stomach and she's worried enough about its return that she has to wait a second before speaking. "We can't stay here." Rubbing the back of her neck does nothing to settle her nerves.

"Come on!" Gareth's already on his feet and even struggling into his coat.

Viv follows suit, although she's nowhere as quick to match him, having to deal with far more items of clothing. Hot on his heels, she's surprised when, rather than heading to the front doors at the corner of the building, they force their way over to the bar. Once there he lifts the flap at one end and disappears through a door behind it without slowing.

Viv looks sideways at the barman as she follows in Gareth's stead, expecting a protest. All she gets is a wink as he reaches for the flap to return it to its closed position. She's only taken a step in Gareth's stead when light floods the place courtesy of the front doors being thrown open.

Looking over her shoulder, a primordial part of Viv already knows who it is she'll see. And she's not disappointed, excepting that she is. Very.

Viv crosses her fingers he hasn't seen her, ducks low and shoots forward through the door, pleased when this is closed behind her. Gareth who's marching down the hallway they've entered disappears around a corner and she hurries to catch up.

She catches sight of him again as she rounds the same corner, in time to see him opening a door, the light streaming in telling her it's the way out. He turns and beckons to her to get a wriggle on.

"Come on." He holds his hand out and grabs hers, tugging her through the door. He then slams it behind them and drags her along the alley as though their lives depend on it.

Any hopes that Kenny hasn't seen her are dashed when the outside door crashes open behind them, followed by footsteps thundering in their direction. These are interspersed with ragged breathing and a gasped out, "Effing bitch." It's all the prompting she needs to dig deep and find muscles she hasn't used since sports day at primary school.

7

Viv's breath burns her throat and she doesn't dare look back. Instead she concentrates on keeping her hand in Gareth's as he pulls her along at a speed she'd never be able to manage on her own.

She comes close to taking a tumble when he swerves around a corner, crosses a narrow delivery lane and takes them down yet another alley. Only some fancy footwork keeps her on hers. She doesn't have time to gather her wits before he's off into another alley and another.

It's as though he knows where he's going.

Only when he opens a gate set into a tall brick wall and drags her into a small yard, does she think he's made a mistake. They're trapped! That is until the backdoor of the property opens to reveal an elderly lady in a pale pink, quilted house coat.

Expecting the old girl to scream or yell for

help, Viv's stunned when she smiles broadly. Gareth doesn't give the woman a chance to speak, putting his finger to his lips and sssshing quietly. She complies, standing aside to allow Gareth and Viv to walk into the house, straight through it and out the front door, although Gareth does check both ways before he steps out onto the footpath.

Expecting the pace to slacken, Viv's disappointed when Gareth is off again at speed, crossing the road and leading her down yet another alleyway. She's now totally lost and reasons if she doesn't know where the heck they are; hopefully, Kenny won't either.

A few more twists and turns and they stumble into another pub and through into a small bar before Gareth finally stops allowing Viv to catch her breath. He even goes so far as removing his coat letting her know their mad dash is over and she can finally relax. It's not until she peeled off all her own layers that Viv drops into a seat at the nearest empty table.

Actually, a quick look around, shows all the tables to be empty, and even the small bar at the end of the room doesn't have anyone standing next to it. However, the rumble of voices through a solid oak door next to the bar tells of patrons in another part of the building.

They're sitting grinning at each other when two meals are plonked down in front of them. Viv isn't even sure where the woman has come from until she spins around in her seat and spies a gently swinging door behind them.

Viv looks up at the woman. "What? We didn't order these."

"Yes, we did," says Gareth, before cracking up laughing.

"Wait? What? We're back in the same pub?"

"Last place he'll look for us is here and especially in the snug." Gareth stabs a large piece of beef with his fork, swipes it through a veritable lake of gravy and stuffs it into his mouth. He then raises an eyebrow in Viv's direction when she doesn't immediately get on with her meal.

"He's right, love, you can relax. We're down a coupla of staff today due to a nasty dose of 'Christmas Cheer', so the snug's closed." Following on from this, she steps over and turns the key in the door they've entered by, effectively sealing them in. "You enjoy your lunch." She disappears back through the swinging door, leaving them alone.

Viv's only just started working away on a thick slab of beef when the same woman returns with the drinks they'd abandoned earlier. These are placed on the table next to theirs to give them elbow room. While it might have felt like they'd been running for hours, there are still bubbles rising in their glasses.

"So," Viv swallows her piece of beef, "You're familiar with the area?"

"Grew up here."

"You never told me that."

Gareth shrugs as though it isn't important.

"And the old lady?"

"My nanna."

Viv nods slowly while savouring a piece of soggy Yorkshire pud. While most people like it crisp, soggy with gravy is Viv's favourite.

"You're sure he won't come back here?"

"As sure as anyone can be, although now people know what he looks like, he might have trouble."

His reassurances are enough for Viv to settle in to enjoy her meal and drink. After all the running, she has no trouble getting through her pint of cider, experiencing a nice buzz as a result.

She hopes Gareth is right about Kenny giving up, because there is no way she'd want to run into the world's best contraceptive in her current state. Never mind getting away, she'd be lucky not to throw up over him if he rough-housed her. Okay, that she could cope with.

She refuses a second drink, conscious she needs to get home, including time to check the way is clear of Kenny. She also needs to ensure her room is nice and toasty before she turns in for the night to avoid hypothermia. When she makes noises about this, Gareth tells her to relax, that he's got it sorted.

"And anyway, you haven't had your Spotted Dick yet."

Despite hoovering her way through a pub-sized roast meal and feeling full to bursting, her mouth still waters. How could she have forgotten about her favourite part of any meal? That's right, being chased through the streets of London by her looney ex.

Leaving the pub, Viv supports her tummy like she's pregnant. Thankfully there's no sign of Kenny outside as there isn't a chance Viv could run as full as she is. She's also a couple of sheets to the wind on the alcohol front with Gareth swaying her into having another cider. Even though it was only a half pint, it's enough to have the tube station looking to be farther away than her waddle is up to.

Concentrating on putting one foot in front of the other, Viv's unaware Gareth has stopped next to a beat-up panel van until he calls out to her. "Where are you off to?"

"The tube."

"No need. Gary, the publican, said I could drop you home in his rust bucket. I'm coming back here to spend the night with nanna. Can't very well run through her place and then not call back for a proper visit."

Viv's wrinkling her nose in confusion when he adds, "Old girl hasn't got a phone."

There's no conversation on the drive back to Eaton Square; mostly down to the mechanical quirks of the engine. Adding to this cacophony of nuts and bolts in a dryer soundtrack is the heater being on full-bore. Without this, the van having been stripped of all its linings would be as cold as an ice-box. Despite the best efforts of the asthmatic heater, it's still a close run thing.

Because of how loud the vehicle is, they park a couple of blocks away from Lady Harrow's place. This way they won't get complaints from the neighbours and if Kenny is skulking around, they're more likely to see him before he sees them.

A quick peek around the corner of the Mews is enough to spot the waste of space leaning against the back wall of Viv's building.

This puts the kybosh on her going in the way she's supposed to. "I'll need to sneak in the front way."

"Do you even want to go inside with him there? He's picked the locks before, hasn't he?"

"After the reception he got last time, I don't think he'd dare break-in again. He'll be hoping to nab me outside."

Even to Viv's drink-addled brain, it makes sense that Kenny wouldn't push his luck if cops are involved. He's been in close contact with too much stuff acquired dubiously to be comfortable around them.

Viv's lost all feeling in her toes before Kenny moves. With him busy emptying his bladder against the wall next to the entrance, Viv and Gareth dart across the open end of the Mews. They then make their way around and into the Square proper without alerting him to their presence.

Viv's unaccountably nervous when she rings the front door bell. Gareth rather than Quincy beside her, she's not supposed to enter the building this way and she's sure this breach in protocol will get back to Lady Harrow, or worse, Mrs Dunning the housekeeper.

"Sorry, Jack. I tried to go in the back way, but my ex is out there."

"Is 'e now." Jack puffs out his chest. "We'll see about that, won't we? My mates at the station will be well pleased to 'ear about this. By the back door, you say?"

Viv nods vigorously until the rattling of her brain forces her to stop. One and a half pints of cider—okay it was Scrumpy—and she's a mess. What a lightweight.

Jack having disappeared back downstairs to his lair presumably to call the cops, Viv feels safe to push the 'up' button for the lift. She even feels safe enough to get inside. She's surprised, however, when Gareth joins her and this must show.

"There's no one home, is there?"

He has a point, but that doesn't make Viv feel any less like she's sneaking her boyfriend into the family home, after lights-out. He's right though. Lady Harrow isn't due back for another week and she's only coming home then because Rupert has a solo art exhibition.

Doubtless, it's being held in a condemned warehouse somewhere in the East End as no gallery worth its salt would want his *masterpieces* within a bull's roar of their hallowed walls.

"No, just me."

"I want to see you safely to the front door. No telling what that bone-head ex of yours is capable of."

"With luck, the local coppers will have collared him by now." Despite voicing this, Viv knows the chances are slim. Just as she's got a sixth sense about knowing when Kenny is around, he's got even sharper powers when it comes to knowing when he's anywhere near someone sporting a badge, even if it's hidden under plain clothes. How else would he have gotten away with his larceny for so long? Not because of superior brain power, that's for sure.

She lets Gareth leave the elevator first, knowing the exact moment he declares the foyer safe by the way he settles back on his heels. Crossing the foyer, however, she can't help but notice her senses are on high alert and she wastes no time opening the apartment door and scuttling inside, beckoning for Gareth to follow.

Incredulous, his eyebrows shoot up until they're hidden by his shaggy fringe. "The front door's not locked?"

"Ah, no. Not with Jack downstairs." Even as she's saying it, Viv knows the doorman isn't up to the task of keeping a determined Kenny at bay.

"What about the back entrance?"

"I thought with the cops already having scared him off once, he wouldn't try that again." Viv hugs herself, even going so far as to rub her hands up and down her arms in search of warmth.

"You know what *But* thought?"

"He thought his arse was hanging out of bed, so he got out to put it back in again." Viv finishes the adage for him. She doesn't get any further, frozen to the spot and not wanting to venture any farther into what she has thought of up until right then as her safe space.

Thank goodness Gareth escorted her up here. Without him questioning the security, she'd have gaily waltzed in without a care in the world.

Other than freezing to death, that is. The inside of the apartment is icy enough for her to see her breath, noting absently how rapid this is. The temperature outside must have dropped while they were at lunch. She thought it was simply down to a complete lack of insulation in the van that it had been so cold on the way home.

"You cannot stay here. If Kenny doesn't get you, the bloody frost bite will."

"I can't stay at your place. What if any of the kids see me leaving there? And we know Kenny knows where you live." Viv doesn't voice the main reason she doesn't want to lodge with Gareth; she's already feeling differently about him.

"Not there, with my nanna. At least until your boss gets back and you're not on your own." Gareth blows on his hands and rubs them briskly together. "And until the bloody heating is back on."

This, Viv can live with. She's already met the woman, sort of, so it wouldn't feel too strange spending a few nights there. "I'll need to collect a few things."

"And risk running into the crazy man, heck no." Gareth grabs her by the hand and she's back out in the foyer a moment later, its warmth a welcome relief.

The elevator only stalls three times on the trip to the ground floor, leaving Viv filling the silence with mindless chatter. It feels awkward until she asks how the kids in her class are coping. The elevator goes from being chocker with jagged-edged topics best avoided, to rocking gently with their combined laughter as Gareth goes through what happened on the tube after Albert had urged her to make a run for it.

"Harry is going to get a gold star for that when I'm back. I might even pull a few strings to see if I can't get him onto one of the rugby teams."

"You might need to get Suzie Cooper a new thermos while you're at it."

"That was her?"

"Yep. Watching that thermos spinning through the air and scoring a direct hit to Kenny's noggin was poetry in motion."

They're still laughing about it when they exit the elevator into the ground floor foyer, although once again Gareth leads the way. Their chuckles die when they see the look on Jack's face.

"They didn't get him, did they?" says Viv.

"No. The scruffy lard-arse managed to leg it before the boys in blue could cut off his escape."

8

Gareth's nanna straightens in her hard-backed chair and grabs the handle of the teapot. "Another cup of tea, dear?"

"No thanks, Mrs Jones. Four is my limit for a morning."

Actually, this is an understatement, with Viv awash after two cups of the badly stewed tea. She's only been drinking cups three and four to be polite.

Gareth's nanna on the other hand is able to work her way through a canteen-sized aluminium teapot of the tannin-laden brew every morning. At least this has been the case for the week and a half Viv's been staying here.

Viv has no cause for complaint, with the old girl taking her in as if she's family rather than a virtual stranger thrust upon her over the holiday season. This had included making Viv welcome on Christmas Day in a way Kenny's mother never had.

It was also nice to have someone to share the cooking with, although it had taken a lot cajoling for Gareth's nanna to agree to this. But there wasn't a chance Viv was going to stand-by while Mrs Jones did all the work.

There's also the plus that the small terrace house is kept at a constant temperature the likes often experienced in greenhouses and saunas. Viv is basking in the heat after the perishing cold of the apartment.

She's also enjoying not having to look over her shoulder every minute. There isn't a hope of Kenny being able to find her here, especially if Viv keeps her wits about her. With luck, he'll have been back hanging around the apartment and Belgravia's boys in blue will have nabbed him. This is long shot, but Viv is still crossing her fingers for a Christmas—or at the very least—New Year's miracle.

"Are you in for tea tonight? I'm planning a nice beef stew." Gareth's nanna smacks her lips in anticipation of a dish she's yet to cook.

Viv isn't far behind in this anticipation, with experience telling her it will be as good as everything else she's eaten since she's been in residence. Sure Mrs Jones might do terrible things to tea, but she's no slouch in the kitchen.

"Yes, I am." She smiles to herself that Mrs

Jones, Bronwyn, has even asked. Viv hasn't left the house since moving in, apart from the odd dash to the corner shop to buy basics. The last thing she wants to do is scrounge off an old lady. She's not that broke.

"That's good. Gareth's coming over, too." The old lady looks sideways at her, which doesn't go unnoticed. It's not the first time there's been a hopeful look cast in Viv's direction with her hostess obviously harbouring dreams of the romantic kind.

Viv leans away from the table and straightens her tummy as much as the kitchen chair will allow. "Oh, my goodness, I'm so full. I shouldn't have had seconds." It's the beef suet dumplings that have done her in. Despite them being light and fluffy, atop a huge bowl of stew, light and fluffy is never going to be up to the challenge.

"I'm with you," says Gareth, letting his belt out a couple of notches and getting a death glare from his nanna. "You want to go for a walk around the block to make room for dessert?" Gareth is already on his feet indicating he's going anyway.

"What are we having?" Viv can't help but ask even though she's full to bursting.

Mrs Jones pauses briefly in her collection of

the empty dinner plates, smiles broadly and states with a certain degree of glee, “Sticky date pud.”

Viv groans. “We might need to make it five times around the block if my uniform is to fit when I return to Lady Harrow’s tomorrow.”

“All ready?” Gareth sounds as disappointed as his nanna looks.

Viv, however, is ready to return to her box-room in Belgravia. With Gareth making her leave the apartment without packing, she’s been stuck washing her smalls every night and drying them on the radiator in her room.

Along with this, she’s been alternating between her own clothes and some of Gareth’s nanna’s. Sure they’re the perfect disguise for trips to the corner shop, but despite not being a slave to fashion Viv isn’t keen on looking like an old-age pensioner either.

In the end, it takes six circuits of the block before Viv and Gareth feel ready to face what will surely be a double helping of sticky date pud. And, this most assuredly with an unhealthy amount of ice cream, finished off with whipped cream and shaved chocolate. But it’s worth it because Viv is going to miss all this delicious cooking when she clocks back in.

Mrs Dunning’s food being of a utilitarian nature and deliberately bland to keep Lady Harrow happy it's got more in common with space food, than cuisine. Enough to keep you alive, but never up to tickling your taste buds.

Perhaps the funniest thing in all of that bland stodge is the old girl doesn't have any tummy troubles when it comes to polishing off a fifth of scotch every couple of days. There'll be no need to embalm her when she goes, with any cremation positively volatile.

The first thing Viv notices on entering the apartment through the service elevator the following evening is that the temperature is positively tropical. "You'd better go," she whispers to Gareth who's escorted her to give the place the once over.

"If you're sure?" he says, directly into her ear. "What if she's had the heating put on in readiness but isn't here yet?"

He voices Viv's own concern, but she's not about to risk him running into her Ladyship, or worse, Mrs Dunning, if they are indeed in residence. It would be a case for instant dismissal and something neither woman would think twice about.

No, with Kenny still on the loose, Viv needs this job more than ever. She wants a decent nest egg saved up for when she goes back to teaching.

Setting herself up in a new place won't come cheap, with a bond, furniture and the like to purchase. Heck, she'll even need to purchase more clothes with the charity shop bits and bobs still in her tatty suitcase not up to snuff for a teacher.

There's just one almighty road block to all of this.

If Kenny is still making a nuisance of himself hanging around the school when she's due to start back, she'll have to apply for a transfer. It was something she discussed with the headmistress all those weeks back.

And the longer Kenny lingers, the closer it will be to the middle of the first term. By then any transfers still open will see her buried deep in the countryside; the positions not filled because no-one wants them. Thoughts of steaming piles of cow manure and not seeing her little tykes again has a lump sticking in Viv's throat.

Watching the service elevator doors shut on Gareth, she's unable to stop her hand straying to her cheek, where he kissed her. It had been so natural she hadn't even thought to blush. Maybe there'll be love post-Kenny after all, something she hadn't dared think about. It isn't like she's pining over him – anything but.

Again this will all depend on how tenacious her ex proves to be.

. . .

There being no need to unpack, Viv gives the apartment a quick search, showing neither her Ladyship nor Mrs Dunning to be in residence. Because the heating is on, she knows they have to be home soon, and anyway isn't tonight the opening night of Rupert's solo exhibition? A quick check of the calendar next to the fridge confirms this and that the fridge is chock full of fresh fruit and veg.

Being alone does cause a flicker of unease, but Viv tamps it down when it becomes obvious Kenny isn't in residence either. It also means there are no duties for her to perform; leaving Viv free to get ready for bed. She's not long turned the light off when she hears clattering in the kitchen.

Her immediate thought is how inconsiderate Mrs Dunning can be at times, but a quick check of the luminous hands of her alarm clock tell her it's only 9.30 p.m. and not the middle of the night. Gareth's nanna likes to have dinner on the table bang on five, meaning the rest of the evening passes slowly at best.

Only when it sounds like someone has emptied the entire contents of the pot cupboard onto the floor of the kitchen, does Viv think she should go and say hello to her boss. It sounds like the woman is ticked off about something, so far better to deal with it now than wait until the morning.

Viv's tying the belt on her bathrobe when her hands still. Does she really want to face her boss while still in her pyjamas? That'd be a big, fat no, although she forgoes her uniform with today technically being her day off. No, smart casual will suffice to pop her head into the kitchen and say hello and welcome back.

Viv runs her fingers through her hair and ties it up into a knot on top of her head, before opening the door to her room and padding along the hall to the kitchen. There's no way she's putting shoes and socks on. And, anyway, chances are the woman won't see her slippers, especially not if she stays on her side of the huge island that dominates the kitchen.

Seeing the fridge door wide open and no sign of her employer, Viv coughs her presence. It's not loud, but enough to see a hand appear around the fridge door. The hand is decidedly masculine in size. Honestly, the woman should think about a manicure, even if she eschews polish. The door shuts and Viv knows a manicure is the least of the late-night snacker's issues.

"'bout effing time you turned up. Nothing to eat in this effing hole."

Any response to this nonsense jams firmly in Viv's throat. While her power of speech might be frozen, thankfully her feet aren't and she backs slowly out of the room. Not slowly enough.

"No, you sodding don't. I'm starving here, bitch."

It's been nearly two months since anyone has spoken to Viv like this and her Pavlovian response is to do what he says. Anything is better than a thrashing followed by other 'pleasantries'. Her feet, however, have other ideas and before she knows it, she's out in the hall. She thinks for a second. Back way out: she'll be trapped waiting for the elevator to arrive.

Front door and hurtling down the stairs it is.

Spinning as fast as her slippers will allow, Viv is off heading for the posh bits of the apartment. She doesn't need to look back to know Kenny is after her, his footfalls echoing loudly through the narrow hallway that twists and turns through the servants quarters.

Despite tripping along as fast as her slippers will allow she's not making much headway. It's something that has her kicking them off, preferring cold feet to a lack of traction.

She hits the swing door out into the main hall of the apartment without slowing and races down it. From the amount of swearing from behind, she knows Kenny hasn't been lucky with his timing of the swing door. Lord knows she's nearly connected with the thing a couple of times after following Mrs Dunning through it.

Good, it's all the lead she needs. She yanks hard on the front door handle and is horrified to find it doesn't turn. What? The front door's never locked. Not with Jack guarding the main entrance downstairs and she knows she didn't lock it.

Damn it, why isn't there a key in the lock?

Turning, she races back down the hall. At least this way she can lock herself in one of the spare bedrooms and scream holy murder out a front window. If she stays next to the front door, she'll be trapped well and truly.

She hasn't made it more than a couple of feet when Kenny staggers out into the main hallway, his hands clamped firmly over his nose. He's weaving slightly and blinking rapidly, telling her the door has hammered him in a big way.

His gaze darts around wildly until he spots her. His hands drop to his side and he fists them ready for action, seemingly oblivious to the blood now dripping down his face. "You're gonna pay for that, bitch."

He walks towards her, his paces measured, each step ratcheting Viv's heartrate up another notch. She soon matches him step-for-step, the only difference being, she's retreating, taking her closer and closer to that locked front door.

She knows she's running out of room when an evil smile alights on Kenny's face. "I've got you now, you slag." He doesn't hurry, instead taking his time and going into details Viv would rather not be privy to.

That he bullet points each nasty deed by punching his right hand into the palm of his left has sweat prickling all over Viv's body.

A quick glance to her left and Viv knows she's only got one option. Sure the door doesn't have a key, but if she can jam herself between it and the bath she'll be safe for now.

Trapped, but safe.

Then all she'll need to do is stay there until Lady Harrow gets home.

Over his game of cat and mouse, Kenny bounces on the balls of his feet, readying himself. He darts forward, his hands already outstretched in anticipation. Viv waits until the last possible second. She's throwing herself to the side and into the guest bathroom when she hears the front door open.

Unable to stop his forward momentum, Kenny sails past. She's not even had time to slam the bathroom door when she hears Kenny and another male shouting. This is followed by a huge thump, and finally silence.

Viv's quietly easing the bathroom door shut, ready to jam herself behind it, when Lady Harrow's cut glass tones shatter the silence. "Who is this vagrant?"

This is followed by someone who sounds remarkably like the Honourable Rupert Smythe-

Brown screaming, "Get him off me. Get him off me!" Based on this soundtrack, Viv has to assume Kenny must be taking his frustrations out on Lady Harrow's nephew.

Better him than me.

Looking sideways under the door doesn't shed any light on what's happening, with the gap simply too narrow to see what's going on.

Do I really need to go out there?

She's still unsure when there's a bellow of pain, followed by Rupert screaming, "No, no! Leave him where he is!"

The suspense is killing Viv and unable to resist any longer, she slowly gets to her feet and opens the door a sliver, all without anyone looking in her direction. Even able to see going on she's none the wiser, unable to make sense of the debacle in front of her.

For starters Kenny is laying full length on top of Rupert Smythe-Brown. That they've run into each other is easy to understand. Less easy to comprehend is why Rupert appears to be starkers. Next to this pile of human misery stands Lady Harrow, her top lip curled, nostrils flared.

If there's a plus in this scene, it's that Kenny is hiding the worst Rupert can offer in the way of family baubles.

But why isn't Kenny getting up? And why has Rupert changed his mind about moving Kenny, apart from the purposes of modesty, something that's been sadly lacking in that individual up until now?

"Your ladyship, if you could hold Quincy, I'll take care of this larrikin for you."

Until he's spoken Viv wasn't aware of Jack lurking out in the foyer with her charge.

The leash handed over to her ladyship, Jack steps into the hallway, ready to grab Kenny by the scruff of his neck. The East London wide boy isn't having a bar of it, shaking his head violently and attempting to scramble to his feet and escape.

He doesn't get far with Rupert lifting off the floor along with him like a freakish Siamese twin. They hover for a second before slamming back down again, the hall ringing with the unmistakable sound of flabby English arse connecting with polished parquet.

It's now obvious the pair is somehow glued together at the chest and places further south. It's enough to have Viv quietly gagging and fighting the urge to speak on the big white telephone behind her. Tonight's dinner thankfully staying put, Viv takes a quick sniff of the air in the hallway. It reminds her of something. She sniffs again, deeper this time.

That's it! After new Lino was laid in her classroom during the summer holidays it smelled exactly like this. Even a week later, the only way to keep the glue fume headaches at bay was by having the classroom door and all the windows open. No wonder the two of them can't get apart. That glue was vicious.

On seeing Mrs Dunning thundering along the hall, her sensible shoes living up to their name, Viv ducks behind the door just in time.

"I've called the police, Lady Harrow. They're on their way."

This news has Kenny redoubling his efforts to get free, ably assisted by Jack. It's all to no avail with him still stuck firm when two cops exit the elevator what feels like seconds later.

"My goodness, officers. Such marvellous service." Lady Harrow sounds as surprised as Viv at the promptness of their arrival. There isn't a chance the boys in blue would respond this quickly to a domestic in her old neighbourhood, preferring to let things run their course. Mostly while they stayed snug and warm back at the station.

"We were following up on the report of a break-in downstairs."

Jack kicks one of Kenny's flailing legs. "And this 'ere is the bloke you're after. 'e's been making a right nuisance of 'imself, 'e as."

This confirmation is good enough for the coppers, one of them wasting no time in slapping cuffs on Kenny. A task made easy by him already having assumed the position courtesy of an obviously sticky Rupert Smythe-Brown.

It is not until his rights are read by the officer

still standing out in the foyer, that the one who cuffed Kenny, speaks his mind. "You mate, are going down."

Viv's whispered "Yes!" is loud enough to have everyone looking in her direction.

Lady Harrow's eyes narrow. "Do you know this person?"

"Unfortunately, yes?"

"She'll vouch for me, won't you, love?" Kenny's eyes are pleading with more than a hint of "and if you don't, you're gonna know a world of pain."

Viv doesn't need to dwell on her reply. "No, Kenny. I won't. What I will do is tell these nice officers about your lock-up in Poplar. The one registered in your mum's name. You know, the one full to the rafters with stolen goods. That's what I'll do."

No sooner have these words left her mouth, than one of the officers hands her a card. He doesn't say anything and Viv's nod is enough of a response for him. Busy as she is reading the details on the card, it takes a moment for Viv to comprehend what the grinding sound is she can hear. It's Mrs Dunning's teeth.

"I always told her Ladyship you were no good. You can pack your things and leave, now."

"She can't leave yet." Lady Harrow's tone brooks no argument. "Run the bath and get your cleaning products. He's your friend. You're responsible for getting them unstuck."

The thought of donning pink rubber gloves and scrubbing away at Kenny and Rupert is too awful to comprehend. One of them on their own would be bad enough, but the pair of them stuck together?

A huge shudder wracks her frame.

She's thinking hard on a polite way to tell her Ladyship to get stuffed when the impasse is broken by the arrival of Gareth. Never has Viv been so pleased to see an individual.

"Like hell is Viv scrubbing those two." Skirting around the pile of English git in the middle of the hallway, he takes Viv's hand. "Come on, let's get your stuff and get the hell out of here."

Gareth is already leading her down the hall, when she stops in her tracks. "Hang on a second. I need to grab something from the bathroom." Getting dangerously close to the now-thrashing Siamese twins, Viv nips back into the bathroom.

It takes but a second to grab the portrait of Quincy off the shelf above the bath and stuff it up her jumper before legging it. She knows she won't be back here and wants a reminder of her charge. She's surprised to find she's going to miss the small dog.

"Bye Quincy, you be a good boy." Viv is surprised when her voice breaks on this simple request. Adding to her heartbreak is him howling in response, his mournful tone filling the hallway and haunting her all the way back to her box room.

She's close to tears when Gareth does something that lifts her spirits. At first she doesn't see what he's dangling in front of her. Only by swiping at her eyes is she able to see it's a key.

"You know that day I met up with you in the park."

Viv nods in response.

"You didn't think I scaled the fence, did you?"

Thinking back on that day, Viv remembers she hadn't given much thought to how he'd gained access. She'd been more relieved he wasn't Kenny to study the logistics of the visit.

"Some numpty on the other side of the square left their key in the lock. You can visit the little rascal when your replacement starts, if you like."

"Yes, I'd like that a lot."

Watching the doors on the service elevator close for what Viv knows is the final time; the giggles hit the pair of them. On reaching ground level, their eyes are streaming, they're holding onto each other to stay upright and their bellows of laughter fill the space.

A reality check hits Viv at the same time as

the cold night air. "But where am I supposed to go?"

"What about your old place? It's not like Kenny will be there."

Gareth's tone says he's unsure of this option and it is one Viv says a categorical 'no' to. She'd rather stay in a pay-by-the-hour-hotel than venture back to her old life. No, the only reason she'll be going back there is to pick up the contents of her wardrobe and anything of sentimental value she left behind.

This presupposes Kenny hasn't flogged all her things down the market to supplement his income. With the place apparently boarded up, she makes a mental note to purchase a hammer before returning. She also needs to pick up some chocolates for her old neighbour. Without the woman's help, Viv suspects she'd still be stuck back there.

"You could come back to my place."

"Gareth, we've been through this."

"What if I told you I moved while you were staying with my nanna? I found a basement flat in Chelsea, a place outside the school district. Would that make a difference?"

"It could." Viv slips her hand inside his as they walk to where he's parked the van.

"What if I told you it's a two-bed place and we can take our time. Start over rather than pick up where we left off at Uni?"

. . .

They stop beside the van and Viv looks up at him under the light afforded by the ornate Georgian lamppost they're standing next to. "I think … I think I'd like that."

Gareth sighs in relief, drops her suitcase on the footpath and drags her into a crushing embrace. Viv revels in the heat where their bodies connect, her head resting against his chest allowing her to listen to the steady beat of his heart.

How could I have been so stupid all those years ago?

Only when their embrace shows no sign of ending and her toes are numb, does she lift her head. "Aren't we going to get in the van?"

"Bloody thing died on me. That's why I was still here when the cops turned up."

His look of disgust is all it takes for Viv to start laughing again. It's not that it's funny as such; more that she's relieved the hell her life has been looks to finally be over. She can go back to teaching and she can forget about Kenny for at least two to three years, maybe longer with the information she'll hand over to the police.

She hopes his cellmate won't be as disappointed with the performance of 'Big Kenny' as the man himself.

Strapped FOR CASH

Taking down the aristocracy, one prat at a time.

Andrene Low

1

All this effing white! Jeez, Martin might just as well have popped his clogs already. Cue the sodding harp music.

Brenda hates hospitals with a passion and adding to this misery, her arse hurts, thanks to a chair designed to ensure any visit is brief. It hasn't been upholstered: the bloody thing's been panel-beaten.

Holding the clammy hand of her elderly lover, Martin McGowan, she can't help but feel responsible for his current condition. It had been her idea to try that particular position and it was only due to her rough and ready mouth-to-mouth that he hadn't snuffed it on the spot. Although, he'd assured her while they were waiting for the ambulance that he wouldn't have minded kicking the bucket in such a spectacular fashion.

The one thing she's thankful for is that it

didn't happen while they were in London, with Martin's heart having the decency to remain ticking until after their return from the UK.

A vision in white pops her head inside the door of Martin's private room. "She's on her way."

"Bloody hell, I'd better go." Brenda disengages her hand and is unable to stop herself from wiping it on her jeans. A quick kiss to Martin's forehead confirms this is also covered in a fine sheen of cold sweat, though how anyone could feel chilly in Melbourne in the middle of a stinking hot February is beyond her. If anything, it feels even hotter inside the air-conditioned hospital than it had outside where there had at least been a lacklustre breeze.

Thoughts of longer goodbyes are forestalled when they both hear Mrs McGowan's strident tones at the other end of the ward, already ordering people about.

"You'd better go, or we might have another heart attack on our hands," says Martin, grimacing.

Brenda isn't sure if he's referring to his harridan of a missus or if he's experiencing more chest pains. Either way, she punches the call button before hightailing it out of the room, managing to disappear into the patient lounge just along from his room without being spotted.

Waiting in hope Mrs McGowan's visit will be of the brief variety, Brenda stares out the large window that allows unforgiving light to flood the room. If it hadn't been an emergency, Brenda doubts Martin would be in a public hospital but the ambulance had come here and so here he stays. His bitch of a wife hasn't stopped living up to her reputation since the first hospital corner had been tucked in using a T-square and protractor.

She's flipped through all the women's magazines and is down to reading pamphlets on prostate health before she decides to bail. Bloody woman's arse cheeks must be iron.

After a steadying breath, she readies to make good on her escape, releasing her long, dark hair from the ponytail high up on the back of her head and draping it artfully around her face. Pulling her jacket on to cover her skimpy red boob tube, with head down, she hurries past Martin's glass-windowed room as fast as her platform shoes and ankle-trapping flares will allow. It's not that she's worried about having a showdown with Mrs McGowan but she'd prefer to avoid anything that might upset Martin.

She'd take that cow on in a heartbeat.

Taking a quick sneaky peek into Martin's room as she speeds past, she's pleased to see a nurse taking his pulse. If nothing else, this will gag the pile of Crimplene and pearls that's spread like cottage cheese over the visitor's chair.

Brenda's surprised at how upset she is over

Martin's ill-health. Sure, he'd started out as a meal ticket, but she's come to care for the old codger. Even the sex hadn't been too bad, although she'll be cautious about that in the future. It wasn't as if either of them wanted to risk necrophilia.

Near the double doors fronting the ward, she hears Mrs McGowan's cut-glass tones. "For goodness sake, if you haven't managed to find a pulse by now, he doesn't have one."

Freezing, Brenda listens hard. Unable to hear the nurse's response, she retraces her footsteps to one side of the door to Martin's room. On hearing him trying to placate his wife, she slumps back against the wall.

"How much longer must I suffer visiting my husband in this, this ...?"

Brenda can clearly envisage the expression that must be pasted on the woman's face. It's the 'poo under the nose' look she uses at the least provocation and Brenda's borne the brunt of it in the past. So what if she was caught swimming in the McGowan's pool in her undies? Martin hadn't given a hoot.

The distinctive rattle of the clipboard being unhooked from the end of Martin's bed follows, then the sound of charts being flipped.

"It looks as though it'll be another week," says the nurse, her voice firm. She adds "Maybe even longer," and Brenda hears a touch of glee.

"For goodness sake, this simply won't do! I'm going to arrange a transfer right now."

The visitor's chair screeches in relief and Brenda knows she'll never make it out of the ward in time. Luckily there's a door right behind her and, without hesitation, she opens it, walks in and closes it quietly before sliding to the side so she's not visible through the tall skinny viewing pane. Her hopes the room is vacant are dashed when a creaky and rather hopeful voice says, "Are you here to give me my enema?"

Parking in the side road up from the flat, Brenda turns off the engine and yanks on the handbrake. The realisation that with Martin in hospital and unable to remind his accountant to pay the rent–that she might have to fork out herself–anchors her in the seat.

Maybe she can resurrect the previous arrangement with Stefano? Tapping her teeth with her viciously long red nails, she mulls over her choices. Under normal circumstances, she wouldn't give a rat's about shagging Stefano, but something about it doesn't feel right.

"Damn!" Brenda thumps the steering wheel hard. "Don't tell me I need to get a job?"

On this depressing thought, she gets out of the car and locks it before clomping down the road to the empty flat. Used to having lots of people around when she'd spent a couple of months in London over Christmas, she's finding its echoing qualities a tad bloody boring. It's even worse with Martin temporarily out of the picture.

Come rent day, Brenda's still undecided. Martin's accountant hadn't paid the rent as usual to the landlord and she hadn't liked to bring it up at the hospital. The upshot is, Stefano's on his way to collect, one way or another, so she's flogged a bracelet rather than pick up some bar work. But she's still loath to hand over cash without it being life or death.

As an insurance policy of sorts, she's put fresh sheets on the bed and dressed with care. Cut-off jeans, singlet top, no bra. No knickers either and, boy, had that done damage to her pubes. Pulling the flap to one side, she can still see some poking through the zipper, letting her know stripping will be as depilatory as dressing had been.

Stefano's trademark rat-tat-tat at the front door makes up her mind. The money is in her back pocket. She can do this. It only takes this short walk to the front door to change her mind. She's wrong, she can't do this and looking at Stefano, she's not sure she wants to take the cash route when other 'roots' could be so much more fun.

It's the first time she's seen her landlord in months. With Martin's accountant taking care of the rent, there'd been no need for his fortnightly visits. She'd forgotten how bloody good looking he is, even if he is crowding fifty. The Italian blood and accent are a big part of his attractiveness but his innate sense of style doesn't hurt either, although he's dressed far more casually than she's ever seen, with faded jeans fitting his toned frame snuggly. His dark green t-shirt is also fitted, leaving Brenda in no doubt about how she'll settle the rent.

Leaning casually against the door jam, he crosses his legs at the ankles, an eyebrow raised. Brenda switches into rent mode, sauntering the last few steps until she's standing hard against him, her breasts squishing out the top of her tank in down payment. It's one he accepts with alacrity, scooping her up and marching unerringly towards the bedroom where he tosses her into the middle of the bed.

"Long and slow, or fast and dirty," says Stefano, giving her the option.

Brenda pretends to consider this dilemma, even though there's no need. Thoughts of being able to go for it without risk of killing her partner, or simply popping his hip, make her grin excitedly before ripping off her top and flinging it at him. She rips down her zipper, in a 'removing a plaster' kind of way, but can't help a small yelp escaping. It doesn't slow her in arching her hips off the bed to rid herself fully of the cut-offs.

"Fast and dirty it is," says Stefano, stripping as quickly as she has.

She's on the edge of another blinding climax, only her second of the non-faked variety so far this year, when the sound of the gate opening cuts through the sexual haze that's wrapped tightly around her. Part of her is aware the front door is still wide open, while a much smaller part is having too good a time to give a rat'sarse. She's panting like an A+ Le Mars student, when there's a knock at the front door.

Stefano looks up from his position between her legs, "Are you expecting anyone?"

"No, no, no," says Brenda, "don't stop!"

Ever the conscientious landlord, he doesn't.

"Is there anyone there," calls out a cultured male voice from the vicinity of the front step.

"Yes, yes, yes!" yells Brenda, the last more of a scream.

"She'll be coming in a minute," yells out Stefano, and indeed he's true to his word.

With the last of the climax still pulsing through her body, Brenda drags herself clear of Stefano and although it takes only a moment to pull on her dressing gown and walk through to the front door, it's not fast enough for the visitor. A grey-haired besuited gent is already making his way back along the path, a large carry bag gripped in one hand.

"Can I help you?" she calls out to him.

He turns and glares at her as if she's done something wrong and this makes her wish she'd left him to it. Missing out on the post-coital glow so she can be frowned at is something she can do without. A year ago she'd have let him leave, concerned he looked too official for anything good to come of it, but hanging out with Martin means her lifestyle of late has been impeccable, with the statute of limitations on anything that had gone before surely over.

Obviously, she's wrong.

"Miss Brenda Munro?"

For god's sake!

"Who is asking," says Stefano, coming up behind her only wearing a towel.

His appearance makes the legal-looking arsehole, even more irate. "I'm Denis Kellerman, Martin McGowan's lawyer."

On hearing who their visitor is, Stefano leaves them to it.

"He's not? Is he okay?" says Brenda, her hands gripping the front of her dressing gown tighter than necessary.

The look of censure coming from the suit at the bottom of the steps flips to one of comprehension. "Mr McGowan was fine when I saw him at the hospital this morning. I can see you're concerned about his welfare."

That he waves his hand towards her relative state of undress, makes her bristle. If there's one thing she's learnt from Martin, it's how to deal with officious jerks like this.

"In answer to your question, yes, I am Brenda Munro. Perhaps you'd like to inform me of your business here?" Her tone and stance are now altogether less relaxed than they were and she's pleased to see him struggle with the change. Jumped-up old bastard.

"Then, this is for you."

He stomps up the front stairs and hands her the David Jones carrier bag. Without uttering any pleasantries or instructions, he retraces his steps and plods down the path.

She's closing the door and locking it, when she hears the gate slam behind him.

Peering inside the bag while walking back to the bedroom, she's surprised to see a present and an envelope, both with her name on them. Any thoughts of opening them are squashed when she spots Stefano lying in the middle of the bed, ready for another round. She's not sure she's up to it. Sleeping with an older gent for ten months has her well and truly out of practice when it comes to sex. If she was to risk another climax like the one she'd just experienced, she might end up in the hospital bed next to Martin.

"Long and slow," says Brenda, dropping first the carrier bag and then her dressing gown.

Stefano is still in the shower, using all the bloody hot water no doubt, when Brenda drags the carrier bag off the floor and onto her bed. She retrieves the gaily wrapped present but leaves the envelope languishing in the bottom of the bag. It doesn't take her long to rip the gift paper away, but her excitement dies when she sees it's a shoulder bag and one that's big enough to nick more than a couple of glasses. It's nice and all, being Louis Vuitton and a match to the large trunk he gave her for their trip to London, but it's not like she doesn't have a dozen handbags already.

And it's stuffed full of the paper the manufacturers use to pad it out to its fullest. She knows from experience that once the bag is a withered shadow of its store-bought plumpness, her rubbish bin will be overflowing.

She decides she may as well gut the damned

thing now, and unzips it in readiness. The zipper on top isn't halfway along when she's assailed by the stench of mothballs. She's coughing and pushing it away when she spots money peeking out.

Any thoughts of asphyxiation are out the window as she whips the zipper fully open. Freed from their confines, wrinkled notes spill over the edges of the bag and onto the bed. By the time she's emptied the main chamber and all the side pockets, there are an awful lot of one-hundred-dollar bills on her lap and scattered around the bed.

She's rolling in them and having a lovely Scrooge McDuck moment when Stefano walks back in unashamedly naked.

"Good god, what is this?" he says, gesturing to Brenda, who's holding up bundles of notes and letting them flutter down onto her body.

"I'm rich!" says Brenda, cuddling a large armful of notes close to her chest, inducing a coughing fit.

"Who is it from?" says Stefano, starting to dress.

"Martin! He's such a sweetheart."

Shoving the crumpled notes to one side, Brenda leans over and grabs the carrier bag in readiness for filling it with her booty.

"There is bound to be a price," says Stefano, sounding less chipper than usual.

"Trust me, I know that."

Brenda has already shoved the first few handfuls of notes into the carrier bag when she spots the envelope with her name in Martin's scrawl on the front.

One of her talons makes quick work of opening it to see a piece of paper and airline ticket sitting snuggly inside. Leaving the ticket where it is, she removes the letter and after unfolding it, scans its contents.

A sob escapes, and she isn't sure who's more surprised, her or Stefano. Brenda doesn't like giving into girly emotions, and sure as hell not when she has an audience. She struggles to control her tears but this is made difficult by Stefano demanding to know what has upset her so.

"It's nothing," says Brenda, hoping to dodge an emotional dialogue, especially one that involves discussing one lover with another. It all feels too much like an Olympic tryout for comfort.

"We've known each other for a couple of years and this is the first time I've seen you shed a tear when onions weren't involved." Stefano crosses his arms, indicating he won't be fobbed off.

Brenda is annoyed she'd opened the envelope in front of him. She is so out of practice when it comes to keeping multiple guys on leashes at the same time. It's an art, manifestly one she's lost.

"It's from Martin. He said he wants to make sure I'm looked after when he's gone."

"Is he close to … ah …" Stefano's words dwindle away awkwardly.

"No! He says if he gives me the money now there's less chance of his wife getting her hooks into it. If he leaves it to me in his will, she'll contest it and that'll hold it up for bleeding months."

"How much is there?"

"Not sure, I was too busy enjoying it."

Together the two of them make quick work of straightening the money into neat bundles and counting it.

"One hundred thousand. That is a lot of money," says Stefano.

The glint of speculation in his eyes is blinding enough that Brenda carefully slots all the money in the bottom of the carrier bag. She talks about banking it, but he advises against this.

"Why? I don't trust sodding banks either, but this dosh will be a damned sight safer in a vault than under my bed."

"If I were you, I'd get it out of the country. If there's even a small chance of him, um, going soon, you need the money as far away from the widow as possible."

"That's what he said too," admits Brenda, pulling the airline ticket out of the envelope to see where it can take her.

Careful examination does nothing to clarify this, and so she hands it over to Stefano.

"It is a round-the-world ticket. Keep heading east, or west, you can have as many stopovers as you like." He looks more closely. "It is good for a year."

2

Still transfixed by the airline ticket, Brenda hears Stefano say "One stopover should be Zurich."

"Zurich?"

"Yes. You need a Swiss bank account."

"Hah! No way will the old battle-axe be able to get her dibs on the cash if it's locked away in one of those."

That's if Swiss banks are as tight-lipped as they are in the movies. Brenda hopes this is the case but it wouldn't be the first time she'd been misled by Hollywood.

"Find one with an office in England or the States," says Stefano, interrupting the Bond movie flickering away in her head.

"How do I do that?"

"Easiest way is to dress like you mean business, walk in and ask."

"They'll see I mean business when I hand

that lot over." Brenda pats the carrier at the side of the bed.

"You cannot do that."

"Why not?"

"Because there are rules about how much money you can leave the country with."

At this revelation, Brenda sees red and abuses the government and bureaucracy in general. It takes a while for her to get this out of her system. She still hasn't finished when Stefano interrupts.

"I do not make the rules. I only know how to bend them."

This comment ensures she gives him her full attention.

He outlines a plan to see the money safely out of the country but it's not one she's happy with. The thought of handing that much money over to him is enough to make her break out in hives. It's not that she doesn't trust him; it's more that she doesn't trust his associates, many of whom spend an inordinate amount of time either acting as bookies, at the bookies or at the track. Their idea of a big investment usually involves the Melbourne Cup.

Unable to decide right then and there, she asks to sleep on it. She sure as hell intends to look at other options before handing it all over. For one thing, she needs to confirm how she goes about booking flights on this unusual ticket and check exactly how much money she can take with her personally. Come to that, she's not even sure where she should go, other than Zurich.

Not that it takes long for her to decide, London being the obvious choice. She's been there before, Jennie her old flatmate still lives there and, with luck she'll be able to stay with her, especially now Sam and Chris are living in Italy.

Brenda again calculates the time difference before picking up the receiver. It takes all her concentration to dial the incredibly long number that will connect her to Eadie's place in west London; it takes a couple of attempts to get it right. After a series of clicks and dead air, it rings at the other end. And rings. And rings.

It's answered just as she's steeling herself to hang up. The line is atrocious, with a killer echo, meaning Brenda is replying at the same time as Eadie's second greeting crackles through.

Hopeless! "Hang on, I'll call you back, back."

She does so, with better luck and while it's still not a brilliant connection, at least now Eadie is only saying everything once. They discuss the weather and how everything is, while Brenda waits until it's polite enough to cut the old lady off.

"Is Jennie there?"

"Still abed at this hour."

"Oh, oh, I'm so sorry. Must have got the bleedin' time zones wrong."

"Stop berating yourself, gal. It's ten in the morning and high time the pair of them was up."

This news has Brenda in a flurry of indecision. Maybe she should bypass Jennie and go directly to the source? The silence is awkward; she makes up her mind.

"Eadie, I'm coming to London in a few weeks." Her voice catches in her throat before she can continue.

"But, of course, you must stay," says Eadie, eliminating the need for Brenda to throw herself on the old girl's mercy.

"Thank you. Thank you so much." Brenda allows her head to drop back, before continuing. "I'll be a model guest."

The rest of the call is devoted to when she'll be arriving and how pleased Eadie will be for some extra company.

Within minutes of sitting opposite a travel agent, who looks to have never left the country, let alone her desk, Brenda has a teetering pile of brochures stacked in front of her.

"Of course, London is nippy at this time of year," says the agent, in a knowledgeable voice. The fact she's looking at a book that highlights everything there is to know about London, rather blows the effect.

"Yes, I know, I was there a couple of months back," says Brenda, unable to stop herself sounding smug. "My, ah, gentleman friend and I flew there first class on Qantas."

The agent's demeanour changes at this snippet and sensing extra commission, she asks "And will you be upgrading your ticket for these flights?"

"Hell, no! Not if I have to pay the dif."

The agent gasps and Brenda knows she's sworn, again. Martin has tried to break her of what is simply a bad habit, but with little luck. It's something she'll need to be aware of if she wants to be taken seriously when cold-calling on Swiss banks.

While the agent might not have much international travel under her belt, she's a mine of information on everything from visas to how much money Brenda can take with her. It's a depressingly small amount meaning she'll have to hand over almost all her 'hope money' to Stefano for him to deal with on her behalf. A quick side trip to a bank, one other than her own, on the way to the travel agents, confirmed that to transfer the money by legitimate means would be slow and cost a lot in fees. Plus there'd be evidence she'd actually received the dosh if Mrs McGowan ever got her tits bent out of shape.

The fees would be more painful than anything Stefano would charge and, anyway, hadn't she already covered his fee in the scratcher, going for it over the past few days? Her gut is sure as hell feeling flatter for all the unaccustomed 'ball crunches'.

With her flights booked, Brenda's next visit is to the British Consulate to organise a visa. The chap behind the grille also suggests she gets a work permit, making her snigger although she turns this into a cough. With the bulk of her money safely stashed in Switzerland, it would look strange if she didn't look for work in the UK and she's smart enough to know image is king.

It's touch-and-go for everything to fall into place over the next two and a half weeks. Her visa and work permit come through worryingly close to her departure date and she's relieved not to have to change her flights. She's been in to visit Martin every day and is pleased he hasn't yet moved to a private hospital, as his wife has been badgering for. Brenda can't help but laugh when she hears this is because the nurses on his current ward are stalling all they can, following his instructions. He knows full well if he's incarcerated in a private hospital, it will be difficult if not impossible, for Brenda to visit him.

She tells him of her plans and he agrees with everything, even if he's nervous about her putting her faith in Stefano to get the money out of the country.

"You should have let me take care of it for you," says Martin, through his oxygen mask, a new addition since she'd last visited him.

Not wanting to point out she hadn't wanted to bother him because he's looking like shit, she goes for a neutral, "Oh, well, it's all settled now," before returning to stroking the back of his hand.

After a few moments of this calming motion, he admits if he were to transfer it through his usual channels, it would leave a paper trail for his wife that was a mile wide, thus vindicating Brenda's decision to go with the Stefano option.

Her tears are genuine when she kisses him goodbye for the final time. There are promises to meet up in London, but Brenda has a sad sense this will never happen. Looking back at him as she's leaving the room, a feeling that this will be the last time she'll ever see him washes over her. It's enough for her to return to his side for another a hug and a kiss beneath the oxygen mask – involving a lot more tongue than is safe for someone with a ticker on the fritz.

Riffling through the contents of her relatively tiny, but incredibly colourful, suitcase, Brenda hopes she's got enough stuff to get her through the next few months. While it would be fantastic to take her large Louis Vuitton trunk to England, the excess baggage charges would wipe out a large chunk of her traveller's cheques. It's still come in handy, though; she's packed everything she's leaving behind in it, with Stefano promising to look after it for her. She only hopes he's not stupid enough store it at the family home where his wife might stumble across it.

She's sick to death of sharing the men in her life. There's always someone in the background threatening to kybosh her fleeting sense of security. And she has felt genuine security in this flat, perhaps for the first time in her life. Her parents were, and still are, useless. Growing up with the constant worry of making the rent or even eating at times has forged Brenda into the survivor she is.

A final check around the flat and she knows it's time to move on with her life. Stefano is taking her to the airport, due in no small part to her disinclination to hand the bag of money over to him, yet. She's keeping control of it until the last possible moment, enjoying its protective presence.

She's checked in and received her boarding pass before she finally hands the carrier bag over to him. Even then, he has to prise her fingers away from the handle, all the while spouting platitudes about how he has her best interests at heart and that he'll look after her. It's only when he says that even with him taking the bulk of it, she's in possession of more money than she's ever had before, that peace descends. He's right of course and when she takes into account the accessories she's draped in, Brenda knows she's good for at least three or four months without having to work. Even without a protector.

Travelling to Zurich is no fun when you're flying economy. This is the first time she's flown long distance without being cocooned in first class as she had been on her previous trip to London. It takes a day of being horizontal before she's ready and able to traipse around banks until she finds one that has an office in London.

For a non-travelled travel agent, the homely girl behind the desk at the agency in Melbourne does herself proud on Brenda's accommodation in the Swiss city. It's a chocolate box chalet with a plump and motherly frau ruling the roost. The duvets are thick and snuggly, making it doubly hard for Brenda to drag herself out of bed on the day she's set aside to sort out a bank account.

She dresses in the grey suit as recommended

by Stefano, for all the good it does her. She can't even get past the guard at a couple of banks and when she does get in the door at another, they're quick to steer her back towards the entrance. Frau Schwegler takes in her dejected air when a foot-sore Brenda clomps into the guest haus, late that afternoon.

Fortunately for Brenda, the woman is a marvel of Swiss efficiency and knowledgeable about how to be taken seriously by the local financial institutions. Indeed, Brenda has no trouble when calling on her first bank in the morning. She hasn't dressed any differently from the day before but is now wearing all her trinkets. Every single blasted one of them. She feels like a walking jewellery store and is on edge about being mugged, but it works a treat in getting her in the front door and, more importantly, speaking to someone in a suit. That the bank has an office in London is down to pure dumb luck.

After depositing half her available funds into the newly opened account, she leaves with a record of that and the account details for Stefano that she immediately sends to him in a telegram.

Delaying her departure, she visits the bank daily to check on progress but the balance remains worryingly in shit-out-of-luck territory. With the bank having a branch in London, and Frau Schwegler chewing through her funds as fast as she's chewing through the bloody fattening food the frau is constantly serving up, Brenda gets the hell out of there before her arse ends up the consistency of half-melted fondue.

This arrival in London is different from her last visit. Even though the flight from Zurich to London is a reasonably short one, Economy does evil things to a person's body. No one is supposed to sit jammed up like that for more than half an hour tops. Also missing is the chauffeur-driven limo pick-up at the airport. For once, Brenda is glad she's not dragging the Louis Vuitton chest around; it's difficult enough lugging her one small bag through Heathrow to the tube for the trip to West London.

A couple of dodgy-looking characters offer to help, but Brenda is nothing if not streetwise. A filthy look and invective-laden 'no' sends them on their way–without her bag in tow. She snaffles a black cab at Turnham Green, elbowing a punk out of the way to achieve this. Stopping outside the familiar house in Chiswick, she's warmed by the sense of homecoming she experiences as she drags her bag over the threshold, the front door is unlocked as always in deference to Eadie's arthritis and her inability to undo the mechanism.

This complete disregard for keeping the

crims at bay will have Brenda looking for a good spot to hide her jewels and spare change; it's far too easy for anyone to walk in off the street and help themselves.

"Is that you, Brenda?" warbles out of Eadie's sitting room, off to the right of the hallway.

"Sure is. Hope that decanter's full. I'm bloody parched," says Brenda, throwing her puffer jacket in the direction of the coatrack and walking into the chintzy sitting room where the old lady spends most of her days.

The welcome she gets isn't what she expects.

"Where on earth have you been? I've been worried sick!"

That Eadie's eyes look suspiciously moist reinforces the old lady's concern. It throws Brenda. Hells bells, not even her parents care this much.

"I got held up in Zurich."

"You should have called," scolds Eadie, leaving Brenda struggling for a suitable response. "But you're safe and that's all that matters."

Brenda sits tentatively on the couch but doesn't relax, just yet.

"You look like you could use a little something. Unfortunately ..." The rest of Eadie's sentiment dies as she looks at the empty decanter in disgust and Brenda knows her own expression is comparable.

"Has he been holding out on you again?" says Brenda.

"The little pipsqueak thinks he can wean me off it by taking ages to top-up the bloomin' decanter."

The pipsqueak in question is Mark, who at six foot three is hardly little, but who singlehandedly looks to be trying to dry out his auntie Eadie.

"Is he around?"

"No, he and Jennie waited as long as they could but they had to leave."

"Where are they off to?"

"Italy, staying with Chris and Sam."

"How long for?"

"Six months!"

"Six months!" says Brenda, unsure what effect this will have on her continuing to stay here. "When did they decide that?" Jennie hadn't said anything about it in her last letter.

"It was last minute. Chris managed to secure a contract for Mark and Jennie was agog at thoughts of all those art galleries. I'm just pleased you'll be around to keep me company."

With this immediate worry allayed, Brenda allows herself to relax a little. "How long have you been living on fumes?"

Eadie eyes the decanter and Brenda can see fierce calculations going on. "Three hours now!"

"Just as well I arrived when I did!" says Brenda, standing. "I'll be right back."

The flagon of sherry is on the shelf in the cellar exactly where she remembers, although the level of this bulk supply isn't exactly healthy, either. Something she'll remedy the next day.

Back in the sitting room, she doesn't bother with the decanter and instead pours healthy glasses for herself and Eadie directly from the flagon. She places it on a newspaper on the floor, as it's too big to sit on the small mahogany table with the decanter and its tray.

They toast each other like old friends with a "Here's mud in your eye", and polish off their glasses in one go. Brenda tops them up again and, having taken the edge off their thirst, they contentedly sip their second and subsequent refills.

Brenda brings Eadie up to speed on her situation as she hadn't bothered with any details in the phone call. On reaching the part about handing the bulk of the money over to Stefano, Eadie doesn't have to say anything. Her expression more than communicates that she thinks Brenda has seen the last of her nest egg.

"But what else was I supposed to do? I checked it out with the bank and they were going to take ages and charge a bleeding fortune for the privilege."

"You're wearing the answer to your problem," says Eadie.

Brenda runs her hands over her outfit, and her face creases in confusion. It's not until her hands encounter jewellery that the old lady smiles

"Damn," says Brenda, mentally thrashing herself for being so stupid.

"I've worn a fortune through customs in the past. Gold is the best option, twenty-four carat, if you can."

At Brenda's questioning look, she carries on. "The purer the gold, the brighter and shinier it is. If it looks cheap, no one takes any notice of it."

"Melt it down and flog it off!"

"Well, too late now. You'll have to hope your chap comes through."

Brenda knows Eadie is only saying this out of sympathy.

After putting Eadie to bed, Brenda drags her suitcase up to the room she'd used last time and unpacks. She's delighted to see the Christmas decorations are still in place, giving the room a festive feel, even though the yuletide season has long since gone.

With everything stowed away, she settles for a snooze. This is more to do with being tired from travelling than alcohol consumption. There wasn't enough sherry in the house to take care of both her and Eadie's capabilities, even though Brenda had collected all Eadie's secret stashes following directions from the old girl.

First thing in the morning, she'll head to the local off-licence to buy a couple of flagons of sherry. Brenda is in full agreement with Eadie on this subject. The old lady is an adult and if she isn't allowed to deal with the pain of her arthritis by ending each day half-cut on cheap fortified wine, what's the point of living?

Despite being tired, sleep doesn't come. Brenda is unable to stop thoughts of Stefano lying naked on a bed somewhere, rolling in her money. She's angrier with herself than she is with him. She should've known better. She's mid-stew when it feels as if someone's chucked a sack of spuds on the bed next to her.

"Gidday, Charlie," says Brenda, to the enormous black and white cat as he collapses on top of her and purrs strongly enough for her to feel it throughout her body. "I missed you, too."

She squeezes the monster hard enough to make him squeak, but not a single claw pops out. They have an understanding and a strong bond. Something she's never experienced with an animal before. She likes the non-judgemental nature of their relationship, with neither of them expecting much of the other.

As the weeks pass, Eadie, Charlie and Brenda settle into a comfortable routine. Early on, Brenda had phoned the bank to see if her money had turned up but being Swiss, nothing short of a face-to-face visit and maybe a blood sample would coerce them to release that sort of information.

She's therefore faced with a long tube trip every time she wants to check in with them. What starts out as a daily exercise soon becomes 'weakly', as all hopes of the money coming through from Stefano, fade. Despite the temptation to do so, she doesn't empty out the account. That money would stay there as a 'tits up' fund to cover her worst-case scenario.

With each shake of a bank official's head, Brenda's blood pressure climbs a couple of points. Even living cheaply at Eadie's she's noticing her bog standard British bank balance free-falling into 'oh, shit I'll need to get a job' territory.

"What does Stefano say he's done with the money?" says Eadie.

"I can't get hold of him. If he keeps dodging me, I'll ring the bastard at home and screw what his missus thinks."

"Maybe the threat of that will be enough."

"Good point. I'll ring him at the office tonight, our time. If whoever it is who answers won't put me through, I'll say I'll phone him at home later."

"In the meantime, maybe you should give some thought to a job?" says Eadie, adding, "Just in case," when she sees the look of horror Brenda's giving her.

Receiver jammed hard against her ear, Brenda listens to her call ringing all the way over in Melbourne at what is the next morning according to the calendar and the clock.

Her call is answered promptly and as expected, Stefano is not in. Brenda has lied through her own teeth enough in the past to spot this behaviour in someone else.

“Really? That’s okay, I’ll phone him at home tonight.”

While the chap on the other end is still gagging, she slams the phone down.

3

Rather than return to the sitting room, Brenda paces backwards and forwards in front of the hall table, staring at the phone and daring the bloody thing to ring. She's rewarded not long after.

"Hello, Stefano."

"Ah, baby, your voice, it sounds so good. I have missed you."

"I've missed you too, Stefano. But I'm missing my money a lot more. Where the hell is it?"

It takes Brenda a second or two to cobble together his stuttered reply. The upshot is that there was an opportunity he couldn't pass by and so he's invested it for her.

She presses him on the details, but his answers are vague enough that she knows a horse race, or more than one, is involved.

"If you've lost my sodding money, I am going to come back home and call round to see your wife, wearing nothing but a smile. Are we straight?"

Not surprisingly, Stefano suddenly has trouble with what has been up until this point, a crystal-clear connection; but Brenda knows the sounds of a slippery bastard scrunching up paper right next to the receiver when she hears it. This is followed by the disconnect tone. Despite clenching her teeth *hard*, she's unable to stop herself from screaming like a banshee, her screeches of frustration echoing back to smack her in the face. She's so angry she wants to smash something. Preferably Stefano. The telephone bears the brunt of it, but being industrial in design, it survives the overzealous hanging up of the receiver.

"Gone?" says Eadie, to her when she thumps herself into the couch.

Its cushioned softness does nothing to take the edge off her anger and so she drums her heels into the carpet with better results. "He said he's invested it for me."

"Oh, dear."

"His idea of an investment usually involves a blasted bookie."

"Is he successful?"

"Bloody useless. If there's a candidate for the glue factory in the line-up, it's a given that Stefano will put all his money on the nag."

An uneasy silence follows as they mull things

over. The quiet eventually dissolves Brenda's anger sufficiently for her to face her current predicament. Luckily for her, she'd armed herself with a work permit for appearance's sake, even if thoughts of going back to full-time work fill her with dread. She's enjoyed being one of an elite circle, that of a kept woman, for the last ten months and it's been wonderful. Sure, she's been bored at times, but no more so than if she'd been stuck in a cruddy office job.

She doesn't know how she'll break the news to Martin that she's lost the money he's given her. Maybe when she's come to terms with it herself?

"What can you do?" says Eadie, mirroring Brenda's own thoughts.

"Office job. Behind a bar. Something like that."

"I didn't ask *what* you'd do, but what *can* you do?" At Brenda's lack of comprehension, she expands. "What are you actually good at?"

Brenda thinks on this for a moment and after a couple of false starts, eventually comes out with, "Does screwing old guys out of their hard-earned money count?"

Apparently it does.

But Eadie's plans are altogether more grandiose than anything Brenda is thinking of. "Why bother with one-on-one when you can pass your skills on to others?"

Okay, so I've got The Initial Approach, The Tackle, Make Him Pay, The Next Encounter and, my favourite, The Hook, Line and Sinker." Brenda taps her pen against the pad. "Any other classes you can think of?"

"My goodness, yes. They'll need to study deportment, etiquette, table manners and elocution."

"Hello, what?"

"Elo-cu-tion," enunciates Eadie. "Rounding vowels, not dropping aitches, that sort of thing."

"Some old geezer isn't going to give a toss about their language if they're dressed the right way."

"While a fine bosom might be all it takes to keep your Aussie chaps on the leash, it's rather different here in England."

"Yeah, from what I've heard, over here they prefer you actually use a leash."

"Jolly good point. We need to apprise the young ladies on what to watch out for."

Brenda's mulling over whether this is so they can find them or avoid them, when Eadie continues.

"We'll also need a reasonably up-to-date copy of Burke's." In answer to Brenda's blank look, she adds, "Burke's Peerage. It's a who's who of the well-to-do."

"You are kidding me?"

"Not at all. The English aristocracy is proud of their heritage and so don't quibble to see it all there in print. It also stops inbreeding."

Seeing that Eadie is visibly wilting, Brenda clicks the Biro a final time and hooks it through several pages of the pad. "Right, I don't know about you, but I'm knackered."

"I am rather done in." Eadie double checks she's finished the glass of sherry in her hand before putting it down clumsily on the side table. "If you wouldn't mind?"

Brenda doesn't need to be asked twice and helps Eadie to her feet and through to her bedroom, although offers of further assistance are refused.

Brenda is halfway back through the sitting room when Eadie calls out, "Wake me for breakfast and we can get on with our planning straight after that."

Brenda still thinks lesson plans are overkill but the old girl won't be dissuaded and seeing as it's her house and all.

Standing and stretching the kinks out of her back, Brenda says, "Are you sure it's going to work?"

"I don't see why not. The odds of covering

your costs are a lot better if you teach others and take a cut, than trying to make it on your own."

Eadie appears unaffected by both the prospect of the teaching syllabus and the hours and hours they've spent thrashing out plans for each of the disciplines. Brenda has to hand it to the old girl though, she hadn't even thought about role-play, but it would be perfect for teaching the subtleties of flirting with geriatrics. Any subtleties being wasted if they were short-sighted and deaf as a post.

"And you're okay with turning this place into ah, a finishing school?" Brenda waves her hand around, unable to come up with a better description for what Eadie is suggesting she do to earn a living. Brothel had sprung to mind, but been rejected.

"Of course. It'll keep my mind off other things."

The pain the old lady lives with is well known and anything that can be done to make life more bearable is a good thing in Brenda's books.

With three live-in students, there's a heap for Brenda to organise before classes get underway in earnest. Furniture is the priority with the few odds and sods stored down in the cellar of no use, consumed by cold and damp. To keep costs down anything she buys will be second-hand; antique in all but price.

The students will live on the vacant second

floor, a sort of no-man's zone that exists between the floor Brenda's bedroom is on and the attic space that is Jennie and Mark's domain. Looking at the state of those stripped-bare rooms, Brenda knows there's a lot of hard graft ahead to get them to a point girls will pay to live in them.

Still, anything is better than sitting around stewing about her lost cash and it'll sure as hell be better than being at the beck and call of some tyrant of an office manager.

Leaving Eadie safely propped up in bed, Brenda heads to her own. Charlie thunders up the stairs after her, passes her and is ensconced in the middle of her bed by the time she arrives.

"Move over, ya fat bastard!"

While Brenda's words might technically be harsh, her tone leaves Charlie in no doubt that he's okay to keep pummelling the eiderdown with those dog-sized paws of his. His goofy look slides into place, prompting Brenda to lean over and drop a smattering of kisses on top of his head.

She doesn't pull away, waiting instead for the second part of their nightly ritual. True to form, he whips his head around and licks the underside of her chin. Brenda gets ready for bed but sees this is an exercise in frustration. Keyed up about Stefano losing her money and the stack of things to do to get ready for Munro's (charm-them-out-of-their-cash) School, she knows it will be a while before she can shut down enough to sleep. Shame it's already after midnight.

Sure enough, no sooner has she switched off the light than her brain goes into overdrive, with anger at the forefront of her emotions. Mostly she's angry for being stupid enough to give her money to that arsehole, Stefano. She'd always thought of herself as being street-smart.

"Guess that's what living the high life does to you."

Charlie's only response is to stretch out more; apparently there are spots on his tummy she's missed while idly running her hand up and down his length.

After anger comes sadness. People say money can't buy you happiness but Brenda had sure as hell enjoyed the security it provided.

The relief at not having to shag a string of old guys, or report to a grey moron in an even greyer office, had been wonderful.

She's back to facing uncertainty in her life, and she hates it.

A few tears escape, making her give herself a psychological kick up the rear end. If anything, she needs to harden up if she wants to survive the next few months. Maybe Eadie is right and it's time to forge her own path. To be mistress of her own destiny and some other crap Eadie had rambled on about that made Brenda's eyes glaze over.

Rule number one of the school will be "Don't

take everything". Apart from it being unethical, it'll also avoid them being hounded by relatives who can see their inheritance being syphoned away. The same rule will apply to any jewellery that looks to be heirloom.

Counting her own stash of jewellery as it jumps over an imaginary pawnbroker's counter, eventually sends her to sleep.

It's only because Charlie doesn't have a snooze function that Brenda is upright before nine the next morning.

"Jeez, I wish you had opposable thumbs, ya little whinger," mutters Brenda as she staggers down the stairs after the persistent feline.

He looks chipper compared with her ragged reflection in the mirror that backs the hall table.

She stops long enough to drag her fingers through her hair several times, in a vain attempt to beat it into submission, and is still tying the cord on her dressing gown when she stumbles into the kitchen.

She slams her eyes shut in response to the sunshine streaming into the room, unaware Eadie is at her usual spot at the table, until the old lady says, "Goodness. Are you not feeling well?"

"Couldn't sleep."

Brenda opens her eyes wide enough to sort out Charlie's kibble. At least this will put an end to the ankle-high interference he's currently running on her.

"I'll top up your milk after I've had a cuppa." The look of disgust this gets her makes her laugh. "Ya impatient little bugger."

The stop button on Charlie's whinging effectively hit, Brenda feels it's okay to pour herself a cup of tea. She picks up the pot to find it empty. Eadie's managed to prepare some toast, although it doesn't take a trained eye to see the toppings look like concrete laid by a dodgy contractor.

Guilt smashes down the last of Brenda's lethargy as she grabs Eadie's knife and spreads the butter and marmalade right out to the edges. A pot of tea follows.

"How do you get dressed in the morning? says Brenda, intrigued and concerned in turn.

"Very bloomin' slowly."

"Yell out if you ever need help. Won't you?"

Eadie's mumbled response leaves Brenda none the wiser but knowing how independent the old lady is, she doesn't push it.

"Have you given any more thought to the enterprise?" says Eadie, before taking a bird-sized bite of toast.

"Why do ya think I'm sporting these? Took freaking ages for my damned brain to shut down."

"Where will you start?"

"Cleaning. And that's all down to me, unfortunately."

"Flo could help."

"Who's she?"

"The char who comes in three times a week to help me out."

Having never seen hide nor hair of anyone called Flo, Brenda's at a loss. Maybe the old girl has imaginary friends.

"Six a.m., Mondays, Wednesdays and Fridays. For years."

"Six in the morning. That'll be why I've never seen her."

"She helps me shower and keeps my bedroom and bathroom tidy. It's my one concession to arthritis."

"If I have to pay someone, I'll need to get my hands on more dosh." Brenda absently plays with the diamond bangle on her left wrist, prompting Eadie to speak.

"There's a reasonably honest dealer in the High Street and you're wearing a small fortune right there."

"I was going to flog some other stuff down the nearest pub."

"Goodness me, no. Not only is that likely to have the local constabulary at our door, but you'd only get a pittance in return."

After cleaning up the breakfast things and

settling Eadie in her sitting room, Brenda is back in her bedroom. Reaching up, she pats around on the top of the mausoleum of a wardrobe until she hits pay dirt. She grasps the velvet bag and lifts it clear of the carved front piece.

Emptying the contents onto her bed, she's mollified by the number of pieces she's accumulated over the years.

She carefully picks through the pile, sorting them into pieces she loves, those from Martin and thankfully, the biggest pile by far, being the stuff she thinks is shit.

After selecting her most hated pieces from the shit pile, she stuffs the rest of it in the bag and tosses it back on top of the wardrobe. Hopefully, she'll raise enough that she doesn't have to sell something she loves, like herself.

THANK YOU

For choosing my book from all those fantastic Chick Lit stories out there! It's readers like you who allow me to pursue my career as a writer.

Lastly, don't be a stranger. I'm mostly online at Twitter, but I'm also on Facebook, Instagram (so many sunset and cat photos) and Pinterest. You'll find all the links either on my website or on the bit about me at the very end of this book.

www.andrenelowauthor.com

RECOMMENDED READING ORDER

Heels and a Tiara - Prequel

Friday Night Fever - Book 1.0

Out of Bounds - Book 1.5

Brush With Fame - Book 2.0

Maid in Chelsea - Book 2.5

Strapped for Cash - Book 3.0

Filthy Rich - Book 3.5 - Coming 2020

ABOUT THE AUTHOR

Andrene's love of writing was instilled in her by her mother, although if her mum was still alive, she'd be smacking her across the back of the head given the direction some of her writing has taken.

It's irreverent, cutting and reflects her background as a stand-up comic. As well as being laugh out loud funny it can be edgy, and even dark in places.

Andrene lives in New Zealand in the beautiful Hawke's Bay - an area renowned for its stunning scenery and award-winning wines.

Lightning Source UK Ltd.
Milton Keynes UK
UKHW021438030720
365983UK00006B/1216

9 780995 138940